QUINN ROMANCE ADVENTURES #4

CAMI CHECKETTS

RUGGED & AT-RISK

QUINN ROMANCE ADVENTURES #4

CAMI CHECKETTS

Birch River
PUBLISHING

COPYRIGHT

Rugged & At-Risk: Delta Romance Adventures #4

Copyright © 2023 by Cami Checketts

All rights reserved.

No part of this book may be reproduced in any form or by any electronic or mechanical means, including information storage and retrieval systems, without written permission from the author, except for the use of brief quotations in a book review.

Edited by Daniel Coleman, Michele Paige Holmes, and Jenna Roundy

Cover art Katie Garland, Sapphire Midnight Design

ACKNOWLEDGMENTS

Cover Art Design: Katie Garland, Sapphire Midnight Design

Content Editor: Daniel Coleman and Michele Paige Holmes

Copy Editor: Jenna Roundy

FREE BOOK

Receive a free copy of *Seeking Mr. Debonair: The Jane Austen Pact* at https://dl.bookfunnel.com/38lc5oht7r and signing up for Cami's newsletter.

CHAPTER ONE

Griff Quinn clenched the back of the leather chair. He stared down his boss, Sutton Smith. Was it possible the enigmatic hero was lying to him? It would be a first. In the three years Griff had worked as one of Smith's security specialists, Griff was certain Sutton had been incapable of untruth.

"You discovered this intel how?" Griff asked, stalling for time. If he could think for two seconds, he could find a way out of being assigned to this job. He suspected it was an impossible internal battle he was waging. Someone could kidnap and hurt the only woman who'd ever punctured his heart. The prospect was dreadful enough that he wanted to sprint out the door and find her immediately.

"Dark web. I haven't pinned down who sent out the request, but it's a million dollars to deliver Scarlett Lily."

A million dollars. What kind of a depraved lunatic offered a million dollars to kidnap and surely do unthinkable atrocities to a woman? Anger churned in Griff's gut. Some idiot had dared to put a target like that on the woman he had once loved—obviously this person didn't know who they were dealing with.

Sutton looked Griff over as if sensing something was wrong. "Baron and Nessa will find the instigator and I'll personally head up the team to take him down, but I need you on this one, Griff, and I need you there now."

Griff looked away from Sutton's penetrating gaze. "You know Scarlett Lily and I have ... history."

"I wasn't aware of that. How long ago?"

"College." Another lifetime. Before Scarlett became a household name. Before Griff had hardened his heart to love. "Back then, she went by Jane Monroe, and her hair was blonde instead of red." Head over heels summed up their relationship—at least, it used to. Griff remembered what they'd had, and he had to bite back a smile and then a frown. He wouldn't allow himself to be soft like that ever again. The military had opened his eyes to a harsh reality. Saving lives was his calling now. Love with anyone, including a now-famous actress, couldn't factor in. Not when he faced the inevitable day he wouldn't return from a job.

"Will it interfere with your execution?"

Griff studied his hands gripping the chair for half a second, then lifted his gaze to meet Sutton's. Nothing had ever interfered with his execution. In college, he'd thought the sun rose and set on Jane. That was in the past. She'd gone on to become a renowned action movie star, and he'd gone on to kill his own soul. They had nothing in common, and there was no reason to worry that she might penetrate his armor and give him something to care about. The only people in this world he allowed himself to care about were his immediate family, his former brothers from the SEALs, and the man standing in front of him. That never needed to change.

"No, sir," Griff said, resolute.

"Good. I'll text her coordinates to your phone. You get there, and I'll have the team in place to remove you both within the hour. Make sure you aren't tailed. With a million-dollar offer, the rats will come out of hiding quick to take her in."

Griff nodded and strode from the room. His heart beat in a weird pattern as his mind whispered the name over and over again: *Scarlett Lily*. But Griff knew her as someone far different from the notorious redhead. His Jane. Good thing staying strong and detached from assignments was never a problem for him.

CHAPTER TWO

Scarlett Lily walked through her Newport Beach home, closing blinds as she went. She used to never close the blinds in her spacious living area. She loved the view of her infinity pool, her small, landscaped yard with flowering bushes and trees, hanging and potted baskets overflowing with blooms, and the beach and ocean beyond. But something had her unsettled lately.

Obsessed fans, occasional threats, stalkers, and paparazzi had been such a part of her life the last ten years that she hardly noticed them anymore. She didn't think it was any of those normal concerns. Her security system was engaged, and the people hired to monitor the gate and her exclusive neighborhood were top notch. She was safe, but she had been a believer her entire life, and if the Lord put an impression in her mind, she listened. Right now the impression wasn't *Run*, but it was definitely *Be aware*. Some might think she was simply being paranoid because she had been the lead in one too many action movies, but she never doubted her intuition.

Entering the kitchen, she pulled out a glass and a bottle of Fiji water from the fridge. Her throat felt sandpapery from all the concern. She poured the water into the glass and smiled. Griff Quinn had always made fun of her for having to drink out of real glass, teasing her about being a princess. Ah, Griff. At the Georgia Patriots' end-of-season celebration, she'd tried to plant some seeds with his youngest brother, Mack, with the hope that Griff would contact her again. She'd heard he was sometimes in southern California with the enigmatic Sutton Smith. It had been weeks and nothing had changed. She still longed for Griff, and he remained out of her reach. Ten long, lonely years. It was pathetic she couldn't shut him from her memories as he obviously had done of her, but he was the love of her life.

She took a long sip of the water and stared at her spacious, top-of-the-line kitchen with slate flooring imported from India and quartz countertops from Brazil. She liked the contrast of the gray swirled countertop and flooring against the dark walnut cabinets. With all the light from the floor-to-ceiling windows and retractable walls leading out to the pool and patio, there was plenty of light to offset the darkness of the wood. Except for right now, when she had the blinds all tightly closed.

In the eyes of the world, she had it all. Money, fame, handsome men constantly chasing her. She could pick and choose which movies she acted in. She preferred action, but she'd dabbled in drama and rom-coms. She hated the rom-coms. There was inevitably a battle with the producer when she refused to do a love scene, but they always ended up cutting the on-screen intimacy because they wanted her name and notoriety. She also loathed pretending to fall in love, considering the man she'd always loved had ditched her for the military years ago.

The truth was that she was lonely. Most of her fellow actors, the ones who didn't mock her for her morality, were great friends to her, when they were all on set. After the shooting ended, they went on with their lives. Her parents loved her and were very proud of her, but they were retired and spent their winters in Costa Rica. They'd come for Christmas a few months ago, met her in Aspen at her spacious cabin, but then they'd gone back to the warm weather. They would return to their home in Canton, Ohio, sometime in April. A month after that, they *might* come see her. She could fly to Costa Rica to see them. She had a break from filming for the next month. Newport Beach usually had great weather in March, but Costa Rica would be even nicer.

She sighed and rubbed the condensation from the glass, lost in thought.

"That's a heavy sigh," a deep voice said behind her.

Scarlett dropped the glass and screamed. The glass shattered on the floor. Muscular arms wrapped around her waist and whisked her away from the glass shards and water spraying every direction.

She screamed again and kicked against her captor, throwing her head back into his chest as her fingernails clawed at his arms. Her attempts to free herself didn't seem to even faze the well-built man, but she was just getting started. She'd starred in too many action shows to not know how to fight. Slamming her heel down on his instep, she immediately regretted not having shoes on. She tried to pull her arms free so she could claw at his face.

"Calm down, Jane." The man flipped her around and glowered down at her.

She stared at his perfect face. It was a good thing he still held on to her waist, because she would've fallen over. Relief rushed through her, and warmth and desire for the man touching her quickly followed. He was here. Griff Quinn. Had he finally come for her?

"Griff ..." She was at a loss for how to respond to the vision before her. "Only you call me Jane," she whispered, barely louder than the pulse still pounding in her ears. Even her parents and college friends had moved on to Scarlett.

Griff arched an eyebrow at her, released her waist, and stepped back. Why did he step back? He'd finally come, and she was ready for an Oscar-worthy reconnection scene. He'd lift her high into the air, pivot while holding her aloft and staring up at her as if she was his world, all the glorious muscles in his arms bulging and her body filling with love for him. Then he'd slowly lower her and capture her lips with his own, and the world would explode with light and happiness as they were finally together again.

She'd dreamed about it so many times. Why wasn't it happening? Why was he staring at her, with his brilliant blue eyes all cold and his muscular frame all tight and military-looking as he clasped his hands behind his back? *Release those hands and use them to hold me, you big jerk.* He'd deserted her and now he'd scared her sneaking into her house like that, but if he'd really come for her, they could talk through all the pain and lost years.

"That's still your real name, correct?" he asked brusquely. "Or did you legally change it to fit in your fantasy world, like you changed your hair and your life?"

Why was he being so surly? The Griff she remembered was serious about life and his purpose in it, but he loved and laughed with her. Long-anticipated dreams were shattering faster than the glass shards at her feet. He obviously didn't approve of her stage name, her brilliantly dyed red hair, or her success in acting. The chill in his blue eyes and his condescending words had her backing away.

Griff reached out and pulled her closer to him. "Glass," he muttered, but he didn't release her. Her breath shortened, and warm tremors spread from where his hands wrapped around her upper arms.

He was fully focused on her, all broody and perfect-looking, with his dark blond hair cut short, his sculpted face clean-shaven, and a fitted T-shirt that showed off every one of his glorious muscles. She'd co-starred with men who honed their bodies to perfection in the gym and never used their muscles for anything but looking good. Griff looked much better than good—he was the real-life version of what her actor buddies portrayed. He could rescue any woman from a terrifying situation and make them pine for him as he stayed aloof and perfect.

Scarlett couldn't pull her gaze from his blue eyes, which seemed to soften as he stayed right in her space. He smelled clean and crisp, but Griff had never been one to pile on cologne and ruin his natural tough-guy smell. She loved his smell and was thrilled that it hadn't changed. She wished she could lay her head against his chest and just inhale his scent, right after he kissed her. They were close again and in the perfect position for that kiss. He was the one who'd tugged her into his arms, with an excuse of saving her feet from the glass. He needed to apologize for a whole slew of things, and he could, right after the kiss.

What was he waiting for? Worry traced through her as she wondered why he wasn't claiming her lips. Was he going to kiss her? What would she do if he didn't kiss her? Why was he finally here, breaking into her house and scaring her like that, if it wasn't to reconnect? Griff had never been like normal men who would knock on the door or beg for her attention, but those were just more reasons why she loved him.

The concern disappeared and warmth filled her as he leaned a fraction closer. Scarlett arched up toward him as he bent down. Both his hands trailed up her arms until he was cupping her neck with his palms, his thumbs gently tracing along her jawline. Her heart thudded quicker and quicker as her skin tingled from his touch. Griff. All those years of waiting, and now he was truly here. He'd come for her, and finally she would feel the pressure of his mouth on hers. He would remember how much they'd loved each other, and they could start all over again—not as innocent college students, but as adults who had been through a lot and were now choosing to be together again.

His breath warmed her lips, and she loved that he seemed as out of breath as she was. She almost cheered out loud to know she was affecting him. She was way past him affecting her. She was ready to forget that he'd abruptly stopped responding to her emails, texts, and phone calls when he was deployed. Only a short note came, telling her they couldn't together. They could easily move past his years of coldness and her years of pain. She could forgive and forget and soften him with all the love she still had for him.

She wrapped her hands around his perfect shoulders and snuggled in close to his beautifully formed chest. He felt so good. She'd missed him so much. Her heart was cheering, *Griff, Griff, Griff*. Her lips were begging, *Just kiss me already*.

"Jane," he sort of groaned out.

She smiled, loving the sound of her real name on his lips, said with desire now instead of contempt. Having him close was heaven. The anticipation of his kiss was about killing her. They were centimeters apart. Their breath intermingled, and she could almost taste the peppermint-flavor of his mouth. She wouldn't cross that distance, though. She knew she'd forgive him without missing a beat, but she did have a shard of pride left. He was the one who had deserted her and broken her heart all those years ago. She'd prayed for him to come, and now he was here, but it was on him to claim her mouth and secure her heart again. Griff was a man clear through, and she expected him to step up and be a man when it came to their reconnection.

He didn't move, though. His hands stayed cupping her neck, his thumbs lining her jaw. His strong body overshadowed hers more beautifully than anything a movie screen could replicate, but his lips simply hovered. *Move those lips*, she tried to beg him without saying a word. She was an expert at that onscreen. Why wasn't it working right now?

His blue eyes had settled on hers, drinking her in. She'd missed seeing that look in his beautiful eyes and dreamed about seeing it again—the look where she knew she was the one for Griff Quinn, the only man she'd ever wanted.

Scarlett waited and waited. "Griff?" she whispered, hoping it would come through in her voice—*I've been waiting for you. I still love you. Please make me yours again with your mind-blowing kisses.*

He blinked as if coming out of a trance. Then he did the unthinkable: he released his grip and stepped back, inadvertently breaking her hold on him.

Scarlett felt like she'd been dropped off a cliff. Her stomach plummeted and her head spun. What had just happened? "Griff?" she asked again. She wanted to fling herself back into his arms, but his eyes had turned cold and he was clasping his hands behind his back as if to restrain himself. The muscles in his neck, shoulders, and arms popped. She'd think he was gloriously beautiful ... if he hadn't just stepped away from their long-anticipated kiss.

"You need to pack a bag," he said. "We're bugging out of here."

"Excuse me?" Her heart slammed against her chest. He wanted to take her away? Why? Did that mean he did want her with him again? If that was true, why hadn't he kissed her? Why was he putting that military shutter over his emotions and pulling away from her? If he did care for her, he was hiding it well and was a better actor than anyone she'd ever starred with.

"I'll explain on the way. Our vehicle will be ready for us soon, but we need to meet them down the beach to avoid anyone seeing you leave."

He turned away. Desperation poured over her like a torrential spring rain. What was happening? She would willingly go anywhere with Griff, but not like this. He acted like she was a piece of baggage he had to pick up on his way to something more important.

She put her hand on his arm. He pivoted quickly back to her, sucking in a breath.

"Griff?"

He simply stared at her. Griff wasn't one to waste words, but this was ridiculous.

She had to know. "What are you doing here?"

He pulled in and then pushed out a long breath. His eyes flickered over her face, lingering on her lips before meeting her gaze again. Hope rose inside of her. Griff had come for her. That was all that mattered. The kiss might take longer to get to than she'd like, but it would come. It was fine to draw out the suspense and make her want it even more.

Oh, how she loved this man. The only man who was real with her, who loved her as plain Jane, without all the makeup and glam and success. Griff was also tough enough to stand by her side and not need her holding his hand. He'd wanted her and loved her, but he wasn't needy and could definitely hold his own in any circle. She yearned for Griff Quinn. No other man had been her equal in confidence and goals and the ability to take life on and come out the victor. Griff was all of that and much more. He was the love of her youthful heart, and now that he was here, she knew that love hadn't dimmed.

"I came to protect you," he ground out. There was something in his bearing that had her hoping still, but it was a very small something.

Her hand fell away from his arm. "You didn't come for *me?*"

"I've been assigned to protect you."

"Assigned?" All of her hope deflated, and her dreams of love were dashed by the coldness radiating off of him.

He nodded shortly.

"Protect me from who?" she asked, hating the way her voice pitched. He had to know he still affected her. Could he have forgotten how much she'd loved him? She doubted he knew how much she'd cried when he stopped responding to her. The military was an honorable career and she respected his desire to serve and protect, but three months after he was deployed the first time, he'd cut off all communication, never responding to her emails, texts, or phone calls. It had killed something inside of her. She'd thought him being here could resurrect it, but ... assigned?

"Sutton Smith received intel that there's a million-dollar request for you."

"What?" Her stomach plummeted, and she felt like she'd been rammed into from behind.

He shrugged. "We don't know the source yet, but the hit is real."

Real. She didn't like real. "A million dollars? To kidnap me?"

He nodded. The serious expression in his eyes horrified her as much as the million-dollar bounty. This was serious.

"Through the dark web?"

"How do you know about the dark web?" He looked her over as if she was an immature teenager. She was an accomplished woman, and even though the action she saw wasn't real, she'd seen plenty of action.

"In *The Fearless Warrior,* they used the dark web."

Griff raised his eyebrows in question. Apparently, he didn't watch her movies.

"The heroine, Average Amy, does a reality show about trying the average person's job out," she explained. He didn't acknowledge that he recognized the movie or her character. "Anyway, she has a hit out for her on the dark web."

"That's where the offer came through," he admitted.

"Why would someone do that?" Her eyes darted around at her closed blinds and locked doors. Griff had easily bypassed her security, both the guards at the gate and her top-of-the-line system. What if those uneasy feelings she'd had earlier were from someone stalking her home?

Griff's gaze swept over her. "You're famous and the most beautiful and desirable woman in the world. Any man would pursue you."

The compliment was sincere. Griff never blew smoke, but the way he said it was analytical—as if she were a beautiful and unique piece of artwork in a museum that anybody would want to steal because it was valuable, but the value had nothing to do with *her*. Nothing to do with the down-to-earth woman she thought Griff Quinn had loved. Lately, she felt like she'd lost that woman, and she really wanted her back.

Her eyes narrowed. "So you think I'm the most beautiful and desirable woman in the world, and *you* would pursue me?"

He gave her a practiced and very chilly smile. "I was speaking in the general sense. Any man who wanted women would want you."

"So you don't want women?"

"Stop it, Jane. Go pack your bag. Unless you'd prefer wearing that for the next few weeks." His gaze swept over her comfortable fitted T-shirt and knee-length cotton skirt.

"What would *you* prefer I wear, Griff Quinn?" She was ticked off enough that she wanted to goad him into admitting he was, at the very least, still attracted to her. Her heart beat painfully.

He arched an eyebrow mockingly, his lips curving in a smirk. "Go pack, Jane."

"Stop calling me Jane." She folded her arms across her chest, her anger, frustration, and desperation deepening. Griff didn't love her. Griff didn't seem to care about her at all right now.

"Forgive me ... Scarlett." The slight smirk turned to a tight-lipped angry line. "Go pack," he demanded in a voice that few would argue with.

"No." Scarlett pursed her own lips. "Not until you tell me where we're going and why I should go with *you*. If I'm in danger, I'll hire my own security." She was tough, smart, and wealthy. She didn't need Griff Quinn, especially not the impenetrable Griff Quinn standing in front of her.

Griff slowly, deliberately walked toward her. He looked intimidating and so stinking attractive. He could give any action hero a run for their money. Even though he towered over her, she wouldn't allow herself to back away from him. She glared up at him, borrowing on years of acting a part. If he could be cold and unattached, she could act that way too.

"I'm sure you could hire your own security, but Sutton's team is the best in the world. His tech guys will find this threat. His team of former Navy SEALs and professional security specialists will neutralize it. And *I* will watch over *you* every second of the day." His eyes traveled over her, and something in his gaze reached out to her. It heated her clear through, no matter how hard she tried to fight it, seeing how he didn't love her any longer. "To make sure you're safe," he added.

"So this is only about my safety?" She begged him to open up to her, to tell her he was here because he cared. Everyone in her life, except her parents, acted a part, told her what she wanted to hear. Griff was real, and she needed to know the truth.

He studied her and finally nodded.

Scarlett shriveled inside. Griff wouldn't lie to her. She straightened her spine and put on her tough action-star face. "I'm sure the famous Sutton Smith has many, many security personnel who could whisk me away and keep me safe. Why you?"

His smirk reappeared. "Because I'm the best."

She gave him a saucy glare. "I don't doubt that, but why would you accept an assignment to 'watch me every second of the day'? Knowing our history, this can't be easy for you." She was projecting her own feelings. Being with him and knowing he didn't love her would be horrific for her, yet he didn't seem bothered by it at all.

His gaze never left hers, and she thought that deep down in those blue eyes she could see the Griff she used to love. He lifted his hand and grazed his knuckles along her jawline, which set her panting for air again. He could have her at his mercy before she could blink. Sadly for her, she wanted to be at his mercy.

"Because I used to care," he murmured in a deep, gruff voice.

"Used to?" No. It was all over between them. She didn't want to be around him another second if he had no feelings for her.

A few beats passed. He pulled his hand back and nodded. "Used to." His gaze left hers and swept around the room. "Nice place."

Scarlett felt unsteady and chilled. Even when he'd stopped responding to her years ago, she'd held out hope that he loved her, that he'd dumped her because he was noble and good and wanted to serve his country without emotional attachments, or something along those lines. She'd been in many action flicks where the hero or heroine had issues like that. It was understandable, and excusable, as long as they came together and chose each other in the end.

Seeing him now, how cold and detached he was from her and their past love, made her shiver. Griff finally coming and then acting like such a heartless jerk was ripping her apart. Especially if some faceless person had offered a million dollars for her to be kidnapped. What kind of psychotic person did that?

"Why are all your blinds shut?" he asked.

Scarlett hugged herself for warmth. Griff knew her so well. Even at night, she rarely closed blinds, preferring to see the lights outside and not feel so alone. "I don't know. I felt uneasy earlier, right before you came."

Griff's gaze darted back to hers. He knew all about her spirituality and intuition. She attributed it all to her Father above, but many people had scoffed at her when she shared impressions. Griff never had.

"I didn't see any signs of forced entry," he murmured. He stepped in front of her. "Stay close," he commanded.

Scarlett's traitorous heart leapt, imagining he still cared for her. Griff used to tease her that she didn't live in reality. If he'd thought that years ago, he'd laugh out loud at her thoughts now. The reality of being in danger and Griff coming to her rescue was something straight out of a daydream. However, any dream or fantasy of Scarlett's would include one essential element—it could only happen in a world where Griff still loved her.

This reality, between the million-dollar bounty, the fear of who might have instigated it, and Griff being "assigned," was more of a nightmare.

CHAPTER THREE

Griff quickly stepped in front of Scarlett and drew her behind him. His touch made her long for him more, even though she knew it was an instinctive move of protection. He was only here because he'd been assigned to be. She hated that with every fiber of her being, but she knew Griff would protect her and she had to focus on that right now. There was an unnerving bounty on her head, and Sutton Smith had sent his best man to protect her. She had no clue how Sutton's operation worked. Would they send her a bill later? Was it all pro bono work? She smiled to herself, wondering how she could worry about silly things at a moment like this.

Griff glanced at her. "What are you smiling about?"

"Nothing." She wiped the smile away.

"Stay with me," he commanded, releasing his grip on her and pulling out a handgun.

Scarlett felt fear pulse through her. This was real. Someone was after her. Griff was here to keep her safe. And now he was going to search through her home. Even though he didn't care for her anymore, he still trusted her instincts and intuition.

They walked slowly through each room of the main level. Griff searched for something nefarious, looking like the most brilliant action hero Scarlett had ever seen. She stayed inches from his back. She wouldn't have minded the proximity if she wasn't so afraid of who might be in her house. Fans had been too aggressive before, and a couple of them even stalked her before the police had captured them, but a million dollars to be kidnapped took things to a new level.

She wanted to wrap her arms around Griff's waist and cling to him, or at least put her hand on his muscular back to reassure herself like her character would in a movie. She had to remind herself this wasn't a movie, and Griff wouldn't want her touching him. The heartache of another rejection from Griff and the fear of someone being after her made the circumstance all too real. She stayed close enough to feel safe, but gave him the space to do his job.

They saw no one on the main floor. Upstairs was only her master suite over the top of the three-car garage, with most of the main level consisting of two open stories. They walked quietly up the stairs and onto the balcony, which extended twenty feet each direction. There were a few decorative chairs and a desk on the open balcony.

The double doors to her room were closed, and Scarlett's heart rate doubled. She grabbed Griff's arm.

He glanced back at her with a question in his eyes.

"Those doors were open," she whispered.

He nodded his understanding. "Stay here," he said in a low voice.

Scarlett didn't want to stay here, but she didn't want to go in her room and have someone grab her, either. How long had the person been here? How had he gotten past her security and into her house without her seeing him? It could've been while she was walking on the beach after dinner. When she returned to the house, she'd come up here and grabbed her Kindle. The thought of someone in her room watching her was terrifying. But having Griff here was such a miracle. What if the person would've grabbed her before he got here? She could already be on her way to some psycho who planned on imprisoning and defiling her. Why else would someone offer a million dollars to capture her?

She focused on Griff approaching the bedroom doors. She didn't want to think about any of this. These situations were so much easier to deal with on a movie set.

The door burst open, knocking into Griff, throwing him back against the balcony railing. The gun flew out of his hand and clanged on the floor below. Scarlett screamed. A large man rushed out of the doors and barreled into Griff. Scarlett watched in horror, certain Griff was going to be thrown off the balcony to the unforgiving slate floor below.

Griff held his ground and slammed his fist into the man's cheek, sending him sprawling, before diving on top of him. They traded hit for hit. Griff had the upper hand, but Scarlett was not one to sit by helplessly. She pumped down the stairs, grabbed the gun, and ran back up.

Aiming the gun at the intruder, she realized quickly Griff didn't need the gun or her help. He pummeled the man with punch after punch. The intruder, with increasing feebleness, tried to hit him back, but Griff shrugged those punches off.

Scarlett's fear turned to admiration for Griff as he effectively knocked the guy around. She clung to the gun and ran into her bedroom to find something to tie the guy up with. Flipping on the light, fear flickered through her as her gaze darted around. What if the man wasn't alone? She clung tightly to the pistol as she hurried into her bathroom and yanked several ties off her cotton terry robes. Hurrying back to Griff, she saw he had the man pinned on his stomach now. Scarlett handed over the lengths of material.

"Thanks," he muttered.

She nodded, not yet trusting herself to speak. Her eyes darted around. Her home had been compromised. She'd always felt safe here with the highly paid security monitoring the neighborhood and everybody who came and went. Her home security was supposed to be top of the line. They had cameras strategically placed outside. The security people for her neighborhood were supposed to be dispatched if they saw anything out of line, if someone gained access to her home without the proper codes, or if she hit the panic button. Obviously, Griff and this man had gotten around her fancy security system and the guards.

Griff finished tying the guy's hands and feet together and commanded, "Stay there." As if the guy could move.

The man glared up at him, hog-tied and struggling to free himself. The guy met Scarlett's eyes. He leered at her, and she recoiled at the blood covering his teeth.

Griff yanked out his phone, backed up a few paces, and spoke in a harsh whisper. He kept his eyes focused on the man. When he hung up, he strode back to them. His gaze flickered to Scarlett for just a second. "You okay?" he asked.

"Thanks to you."

He gave her the first real smile she'd seen on him tonight. It was there and gone quickly, but the offering had touched something deep inside of her. Even if Griff had deserted her and didn't love her, he still cared and he would keep her safe. Any protest she might have had about going with him died after watching him thrash this large man so easily and effectively. She should have Griff teach the stuntmen how to really fight.

Griff bent down next to the man. "Who's your client?" he asked.

The guy shook his head. "I don't know." He cowered away from Griff, as if Griff was going to hit him again.

"How do you not know?"

"I only have a phone number to call to make the delivery."

Scarlett shuddered at hearing herself referred to as a "delivery." How many people were after her? Her eyes darted to her closed blinds and her hands felt slick as they gripped the gun. Were there more men lurking outside, even now bypassing her security system and trying to steal her away to "deliver" her to some nefarious person or group?

"You stay here," Griff directed the man, taking a few pics of the man with his phone, "and one of my men will come for you. If you cooperate, you'll be turned over to the police and arrested for attempted kidnapping, and whatever other warrants are out for you currently."

The man's eyes flashed. He was obviously terrified of Griff, but the mention of police and prison time actually got to him. Would he try to escape if they left him here? Most likely. Luckily, he was tied tight.

"If you try to escape or if you don't cooperate," Griff continued in a low tone that would've terrified even Satan's minions, "Sutton Smith will find you. I don't think I have to explain what he will do to you."

The man's eyes widened and fear flickered across his face. He'd appeared so tough and full of hatred, so she was surprised. Apparently Sutton was well known in criminal circles as well as philanthropist ones.

Griff stood and gestured to Scarlett to walk in front of him. Scarlett descended the stairs with Griff right behind her. He took the gun. "Thanks," he said.

"Will they torture him?" she asked quietly.

Griff shook his head. "We're not into that, but don't tell him." He smiled that beautiful smile of his again. "We have some great contacts with Mexican prisons that can make a man disappear and wish he was dead."

Scarlett was relieved they wouldn't torture that man. She was still reeling from Griff's smile and the thought of being a "delivery." The contrasting emotions clashed within her.

They reached the main level, and he tilted his head toward the back patio. "This way. Don't talk."

They walked out into the night. A brisk wind stirred from the ocean, chilling Scarlett immediately. She wished Griff would wrap one of his strong arms around her, but he studiously avoided touching her. He was not behaving like the hero should in regards to the heroine, and obviously he didn't want to take her hand or elbow to direct her. He kept inclining his head one direction or another, and she followed his subtle directions away from her home and down toward the beach, too terrified of who else might be coming after her to not obey him, or to question him.

They plodded through the thick sand of the beach, sheltered by the bluff on their left and the ocean on their right. Scarlett never minded the sand squishing under her bare feet, but she was chilled. She wasn't sure what to blame it on—the cold night, the wind off the ocean, knowing she was a target of some sadistic scheme, or having the man she'd yearned for reappear, yet be further out of her reach than ever.

Griff walked by her side, not saying anything, his gaze darting every direction but at her. Scarlett also searched the inky night, only broken by the occasional lights of a house above them on the bluff. In contrast of his avoidance, her eyes were magnetized to him. He *was* a hero—tough, protective, perfect—but she wanted him to want her, to be her personal hero.

She sighed, pushed her girlish and unrealistic fantasies away, and kept walking. Their destination felt far from their reach, but at least no one seemed to be pursuing them.

"Almost there," he grunted.

Scarlett nodded and shivered, the wind whipping her long hair into her face. Griff shifted closer to her, and his arm brushed hers. Her traitorous heart leapt and she had a brief moment where she thought he might wrap his arm around her. Sadly, he just kept pushing through the sand.

She recognized the public parking lot and beach access half a mile south of her house. Lights lit up the parking lot. Several black SUVs were parked away from the lights. As they approached, doors popped open and several men and a woman jumped out.

Sutton Smith himself was with the group; Scarlett recognized him from events she'd seen him at with his beautiful blonde wife, a former English duchess. The other men wore suits and looked like high-dollar security personnel. The woman was petite with long black hair and the most beautiful face. Scarlett recognized her as Jasmine, the wife of the famous country singer Kaleb Quinn. She'd be Griff's sister-in-law now. How intriguing.

Scarlett winced when her bare feet hit the surface of the parking lot, asphalt covered in a layer of sand deposited from sandy feet and gear leaving the beach. Griff tucked the gun into his belt and swept her off her feet and against his chest. She gasped, automatically wrapping her arms around his neck and leaning in. This was the spot she never wanted to leave. Finally, the heroic move she'd been hoping for. Yet she steeled herself to be thrown to the ground or rejected again. Griff's body was tight and he was obviously uncomfortable, but he was such a gentleman that he couldn't allow her to walk on a rough surface. Griff had always been an impeccable gentleman, trained by his mama like the rest of the Quinn boys, even if he was gruffer than his brothers.

"Whoa," she heard Jasmine say.

One of the men chuckled, and Griff shot him a death glare. "Open that door," he ordered.

The man rushed in front of them and opened the passenger's side door of the sport utility. Griff carefully unloaded Scarlett into the seat. He stared at her for a beat, then pulled back and shut the door firmly.

Scarlett sagged against the leather upholstery. Her body was buzzing from Griff's nearness. She wasn't sure which was more terrifying—being a target of kidnappers, or falling for Griff again when he would never return the sentiment.

CHAPTER FOUR

Griff turned to face Sutton and Jasmine, hoping that with Scarlett inside the vehicle, she wouldn't hear the nonsense that was certainly going to leave his sister-in-law's mouth. Sutton didn't seem fazed by seeing him carry Scarlett across the parking lot. Jasmine had a teasing lilt in her eyes. Curse the family connection that had made her relax around him.

"Navy told me there was something going on between you two," she said.

"Don't make anything of it," Griff growled at her.

"I'm not the one who just swept the fair maiden into my arms."

Griff rolled his eyes. "She had no shoes on." He groaned. "We didn't have time to grab clothes."

"You'll have to get some on the way," Sutton said.

"Did someone pick up the perp at Scarlett's house?"

"Yes. Do you think he'll cooperate?"

"I think so. Said he only had a number he was supposed to contact if he got her."

"It's enough. Do you have a destination in mind?"

Griff nodded shortly.

Sutton pressed a phone into his hand, and Griff handed over his cell. He wouldn't be able to contact anybody but Sutton, going deep into hiding to protect Scarlett until they found the person who'd instigated the hit.

"Cheers." Sutton clapped him on the shoulder and then walked to the next Escalade.

Griff pocketed the phone and turned to Jasmine. "Will you tell my family I'll be out of reach for a bit?"

"Of course."

"And get a hold of Scarlett's parents so they don't worry, but make sure they don't leak anything. We don't need to tip this guy off."

"Gotcha, bro." She smiled sassily at him. "You want me to give Kaleb a kiss for you? 'Cause I can do that too."

Griff almost smiled. He liked his feisty sisters-in-law. "I'm sure you can. Tell him hi." He walked around the front of the Escalade.

"Can you do me a favor, Griff?" Jasmine asked from behind him.

He paused. "What's that?"

"Give Scarlett a kiss."

His stomach lifted as if in anticipation. He pushed the need for Scarlett away. He'd almost kissed her when he first saw her; he could not afford to be weak like that again. "For you?" he asked, trying to tease away Jasmine's request.

"No way!" She wrinkled her nose. "For you, big bro."

Griff didn't answer. He yanked open the driver's side door and slid inside. He didn't mind being a big brother, but he could do without the nonstop teasing. Scarlett said nothing about kissing, which he appreciated.

As they drove away, Jasmine was watching them with an obnoxious grin on her pretty face. Scarlett lifted her hand, and Jasmine waved happily back.

Griff liked seeing Jasmine and Kaleb happy, but Jasmine should know better than anyone why he wasn't going to be kissing Scarlett. It had taken Kaleb extreme dedication to convince Jasmine she deserved love. Griff wouldn't get there in this lifetime, no matter how tempting Scarlett was. He'd almost succumbed to that temptation tonight. Those moments when they'd been so close were etched into his mind, and he could only hope he didn't get that close to her again—otherwise his iron self-control might slip.

He'd always thought Scarlett was the most exquisitely beautiful woman in the world, but he preferred her as a blonde without all the makeup. Even with her over-styled hair and face, he wasn't sure how he'd resist her until Sutton and his other friends found the instigator and declared her safe.

He drove toward I-5 and went north.

"Where are we headed?" she asked.

"I have a friend who has a cabin in Island Park, Idaho. He always tells me it's open to me whenever I want." He'd gotten a hold of Tucker as he'd driven to Scarlett's house earlier. His friend's cabin would be a perfect spot to hide, and he trusted Tucker almost as much as he trusted Sutton. Even if his longtime friend had been one to leak information, he didn't know the connection to Scarlett or why Griff needed his fortress.

"Will he be there?"

"I doubt it. He has a few different homes."

She leaned her left cheek against the headrest and studied him. Griff found it unnerving. That fact alone bothered him. He never let circumstances or people make him uncomfortable. Scarlett made him want to beg her forgiveness for giving her up, made him want to kiss her until the sun rose tomorrow. Neither could happen.

He cleared his throat. "We've got a long drive. Why don't you sleep?"

Her eyebrows arched up. "Not really tired."

He wanted her to sleep. He wanted to drive uninterrupted, and he didn't want her looking at him. He really wanted to put his hand on her bare knee, but that wasn't going to happen. Apparently, her sleeping wasn't going to happen, either.

He ignored his stupid desires and sped up to see if anyone seemed to be tailing them. Keeping one eye on the rearview, he sped up to fifteen miles over the speed limit and left most cars far behind.

When Scarlett spoke, he was startled from his world of security by the beautiful woman sitting beside him. "Would you be tired after finding out you're a target for kidnapping, watching your former boyfriend pummel an intruder in your home, and then being told you were going to Island Park, Idaho, for who knows how long with only a T-shirt and skirt on? How cold is it in Island Park, anyway?" She gave an exaggerated shiver.

Griff almost smiled. Luckily, he caught himself. He'd forgotten how ... cute she was. Maybe cute wasn't the right word—most men considered her the epitome of sex appeal—but she still had an air of innocence about her. He'd seen a video clip where a fellow actor had said with disgust in his voice, "Scarlett Lily would rather go to church than to bed." It had made Griff irrationally happy to know she was still committed to waiting for marriage like she had been back in college, and he'd wanted to thump the guy for trying to get her into bed.

Griff could understand why she'd be irresistible to a lot of men. He tried not to think about that much, but he had to focus on a man who was willing to pay a million dollars to kidnap Scarlett, try to get inside the guy's mindset so Griff could protect her. He imagined what would've happened if Sutton hadn't discovered the intel and sent him straight to Scarlett tonight. That man ... waiting in her bedroom. Griff's shoulders tightened.

Scarlett reached over and massaged at the furrow in his brow. Griff yanked on the steering wheel, almost taking out the minivan in the next lane.

"What are you doing?" he demanded.

Scarlett pulled her hand back quickly. "You looked so upset. I was just trying to help you relax."

"Well, don't help me relax while I'm driving down the freeway."

"Can I help you relax another time?" she asked.

He glanced at her. Her clear green eyes reminded him of why he'd fallen so hard for her in college. She was more beautiful inside than outside. The kindness and sincerity that emanated from her used to take his breath away. Scarlett had loved him so completely that he'd known, even back in college, that he wasn't worthy of her ardor and devotion. Yet he'd allowed himself to bask in it, to bask in time spent with her. It was weak of him. He knew his path would be military and that he needed to go save the world. He pushed a hand through his short hair. That had turned out to be naïve of him. Sometimes he wondered if he'd hurt more innocent people than he'd helped. He'd lost the woman he loved, by his own choice. Now he had nothing but his focus of saving lives through Sutton, maybe someday gaining the redemption he yearned for. He couldn't "relax."

"No," he said shortly. Checking his rearview, he didn't see any vehicles that had consistently trailed behind him. He slowed down to change the flow around him.

"When did you become so—abrupt?"

Griff laughed. She was too kind to even tell him what a jerk he was. "I've spoken more today than I have the past month." And truthfully, he was softer with her than he was with anyone, besides his mama and his nephew, Tate.

Her lips curved. "Really? So you're saying I bring out the best in you?"

He shook his head, not ready or willing to play this game. "I'm saying you should try to rest. It's almost sixteen hours' drive time."

"You're kidding." She straightened in her seat. "I'm going to be stuck in this car for sixteen hours?"

"With me as your travel buddy." He pumped his eyebrows at her, feeling more playful than he had in ... ten years, to be exact.

She held up her hands. "You got me. I'll try to sleep." She eyed him. "How are we going to keep those lovely baby blues of yours propped open?"

Griff was afraid his cheeks were going to hurt from these smiling episodes. She'd always loved his bright blue eyes. How was he going to stay focused on who he was and his purpose if this op lasted very long? "Don't worry about me, Jane."

She'd told him earlier not to call her Jane, but she didn't protest again. "Because you're some big military man who's *too tough for sleep.*" She made her voice all gruff and low.

"Fools mock, but they shall mourn."

"*You're* quoting the Bible?"

The playfulness fizzled. He focused on the road, changing lanes as the transfer to I-15 came up. "Won't happen again," he said.

She arched her eyebrows but didn't question his agnostic comment. "Why didn't we fly?"

"Lots of reasons," he grunted.

"Such as?"

Griff glanced at her. Was she just trying to fill the silence, or was she ticked that a princess like her had to be stuck in a vehicle for sixteen hours with the likes of him? He started ticking off the reasons: "Sutton's jets were both deployed elsewhere when we needed to leave. Flying commercially or even chartering a jet, there's the risk of someone seeing you and leaking it. And if we have to bug out of our safe location, I want the Escalade with bulletproof windows and every gadget to protect us."

Scarlett arched an eyebrow. "Did that wear you out?"

"What?"

"Talking for so long?"

Griff rolled his eyes, even though her sarcasm was kind of cute. "Get some rest."

"Whatever you say, bossy."

They drove in silence for a while, and he hoped she'd drifted off. When he glanced over at her, her head was facing him, her cheek leaning against the seat. She was much too beautiful. Her eyes fluttered open. He quickly averted his gaze and sped up again to dodge around some traffic and see if they had a tail. He hadn't seen anything yet, and he knew Sutton would have different vehicles following him through the phone he now carried for the next few hours to make certain nobody was on to them.

Scarlett laid her hand on his forearm, and he cursed and pulled away from her soft fingers. "Don't do that."

"Why not?"

"I need to focus on driving, and your touch—" He bit his tongue. He'd dug himself into a hole on this one.

"Drives you to distraction?" She grinned, much too full of herself. He supposed that was inevitable with the attention she always received.

"Something like that," he muttered.

"What happened to you in the military, Griff?"

He sucked in a breath and almost cursed again. His mama would not be happy with him right now. "We're not going there, Jane."

The only sound was the rumbling of the road and the occasional horn or squeal of tires. Maybe he should turn on the radio. He didn't care much about music, but at least she wouldn't think they needed to talk to fill the silence. Long minutes passed, and she didn't speak.

"So this is us now." She broke the silence, right when he was thinking this talking episode was over. Why did she do that?

"Excuse me?" he asked. What did she mean, "us"? He used to dream of an "us" with her, but he was far removed from it now. He had to be.

"You and I. We've been reduced to tiptoeing around the truth and not trusting each other. That's us now?"

He swallowed hard and made sure his voice was even harder. "There is no us, Scarlett. The sooner you realize that, the easier the next few weeks will go."

He heard her suck in a breath and felt her stiffen beside him. It had been a jerk thing to say, but that's who he was and he made no apologies about it to anyone. Why did his Jane, who wasn't his Jane any longer, make him feel like he should grovel and be soft like one of his sappy brothers would be? Millions of men would give up anything for a chance with Scarlett Lily. Not him. Not anymore.

He focused on the road and the thick traffic around him. Ignoring Scarlett suddenly became his highest priority, and his only chance to survive the next few weeks with his armor intact.

CHAPTER FIVE

Scarlett couldn't sleep, and the hours of staring out the window at the dark night and the traffic flowing with them stretched on and on. She snuck glances at Griff occasionally, but he'd made it crystal clear that she shouldn't talk to him. She'd questioned many times why she'd fallen in love with such a hard man, but part of his appeal was how tough and real he was. There was no posturing with Griff; there were no half-truths. You got all of him, and he was as manly as they came. He'd always treated her with respect—he was too much of a gentleman to ever physically hurt a lady—but emotionally, he could devastate her within seconds.

There is no us played through her head. Maybe he'd killed their relationship in his mind, but she never had. If she truly had to spend the next few weeks with him, she might go insane with longing and frustration. In college, he'd been soft for her. What if that man had been transformed by the harshness of the military and never returned to her? She rolled her eyes at herself, knowing she was making this into a movie. Griff would laugh at her if he knew. He used to tease that her living in fantasy land was really cute, asking her to tell Peter Pan and the tooth fairy hello as they flew by. He hadn't laughed at all tonight. Would she ever hear his laughter again?

They cleared the lights and traffic of Vegas and continued north. Scarlett needed to use the restroom, her throat was scratchy from no water, and her rear was killing her from sitting for so long. She wasn't used to inactivity.

"You okay?" Griff asked.

He hadn't spoken to her in hours, and she appreciated that he was trying to take care of her needs, though his voice wasn't soft by any means. "I could use a restroom," she admitted.

He nodded. "Can you make St. George?"

She wanted to ask how far. She knew St. George was in southern Utah. It couldn't be too much farther. She didn't want to be a wimp around him, but she'd gotten used to her every need being met as the superstar. She tried to never demand, but if she made a soft request, people came running. "Sure," she said.

"We'll stay the night there."

Stretching out in a bed sounded nice. Being alone in a hotel room with Griff Quinn? Her stomach heated up, and she had to look out the window again. There wasn't much to see, as they were going through a stretch of desert in the middle of the night and the traffic was intermittent. The clock on the dash said 12:34 a.m.

Scarlett crossed her legs, shifting uncomfortably in the seat. She caught Griff looking at her.

"You'll be okay?" His voice was a little bit softer than before.

"I play an action hero. I'm tough."

He chuckled softly. Scarlett hadn't heard him laugh for so many years. Her heart cracked wide open at the sound. She loved his deep laugh.

"You may look tough on the screen, but you're a princess," he said.

Scarlett's jaw dropped and she poked him in the side. He used to always tease her about being a princess. "You take that back."

His laughter deepened. "Or what?"

"Or I'll tickle you." Griff had been a pretty serious guy even before the military, but even he had vulnerabilities. If she feathered her fingertips along his abdomen, he'd laugh.

"Don't you dare." His voice had become steel, but Scarlett sensed an underlying humor in it. He remembered the fun they used to have just like she did.

"Oh, I dare." She made to reach for his stomach, and he immediately blocked her with his forearm. She veered her hand back and trailed her fingertips down his side.

Griff let out a blast of laughter that filled the entire vehicle. "Stop," he said, but crazily enough, he didn't reach for her hand or attempt to stop her.

Emboldened, Scarlett feathered her fingers down his side and along his abs. She'd always loved Griff's build, but she was pretty certain he hadn't had this many grooved muscles back in college. Griff's laughter changed to a low moan that caught her off guard. She flattened her hand on his abdomen and simply savored the connection to him. His body was perfect, but it was the thrill of touching him, of him letting her touch him, that had fire racing through her.

Griff grabbed her hand and pushed it away, abruptly stopping her wanton thoughts. He pushed her hand back to her side of the vehicle. She was pretty sure he meant to simply keep her from touching him, but as he placed her hand down, the back of his hand grazed her bare knee. He released her hand, and slowly his fingers danced along her leg until his large palm covered her knee.

Silence settled within the vehicle, loaded with tension she didn't know how to deal with. Griff kept his hand on her knee, and as she battled her growing thirst for him, he said quietly, "You always had the most perfect legs."

"Th-thank you," she squeaked out from a very dry throat.

His hand caressed her knee for the briefest of seconds, and the vehicle could have exploded with the heat she felt. Griff abruptly pulled away and clamped both palms onto the steering wheel.

They drove without speaking for much too long. Scarlett wanted to demand to know how he could touch her like that if there was "no us," but she didn't want him to withdraw from her for another ten years. Yet it seemed he already was shutting down.

"I apologize," he finally muttered.

"For?" *No! Don't apologize, you heartless jerk.*

"I would never become involved with a client."

The fire from minutes before turned to ice. "I'm not paying you, so I'm not your client," she threw at him.

"We'll bill you later." He actually smiled.

"You do that."

He reached over and squeezed her leg before returning his hands to the steering wheel. Scarlett had never been so confused in her life. She had to somehow get through this with her sanity intact. Griff Quinn was messing with her heart and mind, but sadly, that was nothing new.

When the signs for St. George exits appeared, Scarlett gave a little cheer. "Finally!"

Griff could not stop himself from smiling. What was she *doing* to him? Six hours since he'd first seen her again and he was touching her leg, laughing while she tickled him, and smiling like an idiotic sap. He might as well call his brother Kaleb and ask him to compose a love song for him. Pathetic.

"Longer than I wanted," he admitted, "but if I'd stopped in Vegas or Mesquite and carried you barefoot through a casino, someone might've recognized you."

"I don't mind you carrying me."

Griff clung to the steering wheel and refused to respond to that. When he'd carried her through that parking lot to the SUV earlier tonight, it had stirred far too much inside of him. He wouldn't mind carrying her a long, long way, but thankfully they'd been able to avoid Las Vegas.

He parked in a stall that wasn't under a direct parking lot light, but it still gave him a clear line of sight through the glass doors and windows of the hotel's lobby to the check-in desk. "Stay here," he instructed. "I'll check in. I don't want anyone seeing you."

"You don't want all this sparkle and shine noticed?" She winked at him.

Griff focused on her beautiful face for a few seconds. His shoulders dropped and he had the insane urge to cup her cheek with his palm. "No, I don't." He hurried to jump out of the vehicle, then shut the door and clicked the lock button.

The young man checking him in was much too slow for Griff's liking. He kept glancing back to check on Scarlett, but it was after two a.m., so the parking lot and lobby were quiet.

"Everything okay, sir?"

Griff glanced at the clerk. He looked barely old enough to shave. "Fine."

The kid finally found them a room and ran one of the many credit cards Griff had for jobs like this, but then he took another full minute to program keys. As Griff took the keys, he saw a flash of movement out of the corner of his eye.

He spun, and his stomach churned. A man was standing in front of the Escalade, staring at Scarlett. No! Griff ran through the lobby and slipped between the slowly-opening automatic doors. The man didn't even turn as Griff approached, so focused was he on Scarlett. Griff plowed into him and tackled him onto the cement.

The man cried out in surprise, then put his hands over his head. "Don't hurt me," he begged.

"Who are you?" Griff demanded as he flipped the man over onto his stomach, pressed one knee into his back, and ripped his arms behind him.

"J-john Wilcox," he squeaked out, his face digging into the cement walkway.

Griff almost smacked him in the head, but he restrained. "Not your name. Why are you here?"

"The, uh, banking convention."

"The truth!" Griff roared. His heart raced. Had another hit man found Scarlett? The guy was in a rumpled suit but was otherwise clean-cut, balding, and looked like a banker. He seemed truly terrified, but even hardened criminals got terrified when Griff zeroed in on them.

Scarlett's door opened, but Griff yelled at her, "Stay back!"

"Should I call the police?" The question came from the other direction. It was the desk clerk.

"Not yet," Griff said. "Get back inside."

The kid looked terrified. "I meant to help him." He pointed at the man under Griff's power.

Griff growled. "I'm private security. I'll show you my badge later." He had all manner of badges to fit different circumstances. "Get back inside!"

The kid scurried away. Griff hoped he wouldn't call the police until he was certain what kind of a threat this man was, who had sent him, and that Scarlett was hidden away in the hotel room. Then he would have no issue turning the guy over to the authorities. Sutton always made sure they worked within the parameters of the law, and they were respected by the authorities and treated them with respect also.

The man under his knee whimpered, drawing Griff's attention. "I was just looking at Scarlett Lily. I'm sorry."

Scarlett hadn't obeyed him about staying in the vehicle. She slowly approached them and touched Griff's arm. Her touch had the crazy effect of soothing him. He didn't want to be soothed right now. He wanted to beat the truth out of this guy.

"I don't think he's after me," she said quietly. "I think he was just shocked to see someone famous."

The guy craned his neck to look at her again. "I loved you in *False Identity*," he said with a voice full of worship. "My wife and I are your biggest fans."

"Thank you," Scarlett said, grace and poise and all things lovely.

Griff rolled his eyes. "Why are you out at two a.m.?" he asked the man.

The man shifted underneath him and grunted when Griff pressed harder with his knee. "I drove to Mesquite to play blackjack as soon as the conference ended this afternoon and just got back. Don't tell my wife."

Griff shook his head. *Don't tell my wife?* He didn't care about the guy's wife. Maybe this loser really was innocent.

"Griff." Scarlett gently massaged his arm, and the connection to his bare flesh almost overwhelmed him. He could not believe what a wimp he was when it came to this woman. "I think he's telling the truth."

"This is not a movie set; this is real life," he shot at her. "You aren't some human lie detector." That was a part she'd played recently. To his detriment, he'd never missed one of her movies. If he was deep undercover when one came out, he bought it on Amazon Prime the day he returned home. When she'd referred to her role in *The Fearless Warrior,* Average Amy, he'd known exactly what she was talking about, but he'd kept his face impassive. He'd messed up now, revealing he'd seen her latest show.

Scarlett didn't pull her hand back. He was impressed with her bravery, tenacity, and gentleness. "You always trusted my intuition."

He studied her for a beat. She was right. He had.

"You're going to draw more attention to us if the police scream in here. Other people might come out and see me. The police will have to question me. I feel this man is telling us the truth. He gambled all night and is going to have to face his wife when he gets home from his conference. Where are you from?" she asked the man.

"Preston, Idaho," the guy kind of gasped out.

"I'm sure it's a nice spot," Scarlett said.

"It is. I have four boys who help me on our little farm, and I work at the bank in town. My wife makes edible flowers. Have you ever tasted one, Scarlett?"

"I have. What a talented lady your wife must be," she said.

Griff rolled his eyes, jumped to his feet, and pulled the man up with him. "Give me your wallet," he demanded.

"Griff?" Scarlett's eyes widened.

"I lost all my cash, but I can give you my credit cards," the man said obediently.

"I'm not going to rob you; I want to see the address on your driver's license."

"Oh."

Griff released one of the man's arms, letting him fish out his wallet and hand it over. Griff flipped it open and tried to yank the driver's license out with one hand. Scarlett moved in closer, and her soft, clean scent about took him down. Dang her for being so appealing. She plucked the wallet from his hand and pulled out the driver's license, holding it up for him to see: John Eyring Wilcox, 800 East 85 North, Preston, Idaho.

"Thanks," Griff said to Scarlett.

She slipped the driver's license back in and handed the wallet to the man. "Will you please not tell anyone you saw me?" Scarlett asked.

"B-but my wife, my boys. They'll be so excited."

Griff still had a grip on the guy's arm, and he could easily break that arm to threaten him into submission. The man was so caught up in Scarlett that he didn't seem to realize the danger that Griff posed to him.

"Please." Scarlett batted her eyelashes at him, and the guy stared at her like he'd seen heaven.

Griff felt a surge of jealousy rip through him, similar to every time he saw her kiss another actor in a show. It was stupid and irrational and he forced it away.

"I will for you, Scarlett."

"You're going to trust him to not go blabbing he saw Scarlett Lily?" Griff asked Scarlett.

"I'd do anything for her," the man said, still staring in awe at Scarlett.

"What option do we have?" Scarlett asked.

Griff whipped the man around to face him so he could intimidate him. As a bonus, the idiot was no longer fawning over Scarlett. "You breathe a word of this encounter to anyone, I will hunt you down and I will break both of your arms. Do you believe me?"

The man nodded, his mouth slightly open and his face stricken with terror.

"Go," Griff growled at him, finally releasing his arm.

The man scurried past them, his gaze darting to Scarlett.

"Thank you," she said.

He smiled tremulously at her.

Griff watched him go, shoving his hand through his hair. "Get back in the car so I can deal with the clerk now."

"You don't just boss me around." Scarlett put her hands on her hips and tossed her long hair. "And you didn't need to threaten that man."

Griff marched toward her. She backed up, bumping against the Escalade. He planted his hands on either side of the hood and glared down at her. "Do you have any clue what the man who offered a million dollars for you will do to you if he finds you?"

Scarlett swallowed, and Griff's eyes were drawn to her lovely neck. He used to love kissing her neck. What he wouldn't give to brush his lips across that throbbing pulse point. He cursed himself and focused on Scarlett, arching an eyebrow, intent on showing her how naïve she was behaving.

"That man was innocent." She gave him a sassy look.

Griff couldn't remember when anyone but a family member had dared to stand up to him. Scarlett was braver than the heroines she portrayed. Man, that was sexy. "He probably was," Griff agreed. "But the men who will kidnap you and the man bribing them to are not."

She didn't say anything, but the fear in her green eyes hurt him.

He looked over her beautiful face and her smooth neck and shoulders, unable to stand the thought of someone taking advantage of her. "Please help me protect you."

Scarlett met his gaze. Griff wished with everything in him he could press against her and kiss her good and long. Maybe the memories of kissing her and the tension arcing between them were all blown out of proportion in his mind. Maybe if he kissed her, he'd realize she was simply another woman who couldn't affect him, just a job to get through and protect. And maybe Santa Claus would bring him a real pony like he'd asked for when he was six. He'd gotten a fake lame one instead. That's what any relationship with a woman besides Scarlett was for him—fake and lame.

She finally nodded. Griff straightened. Right now he could easily take her elbow or her arm in his hand; it would probably even be acceptable to wrap his arm around her small waist. He gritted his teeth, resisted the desire rushing through him, and stalked around the Escalade, opening her door.

Scarlett walked past him, leaving her clean scent in her wake. She slid inside, and his gaze was riveted as her skirt slid up on her thigh. He knew how it felt to touch that leg.

He shook his head and clutched the doorframe tightly. It was either that or drag her back out of the vehicle and kiss her good and long. "I'll be right back," he grunted out.

"Okay."

She looked so small and beautiful sitting in the large sport utility. He didn't want to leave her for a second. He shook his head. He really needed some food and sleep; he was getting delusional. Shutting the door, he hurried to make sure the clerk wouldn't be a problem. Then he needed to call Sutton and make him aware of the breach so he could monitor it. Food and sleep weren't going to happen for a while—if it was even possible for him to sleep with Scarlett in the same room as him.

He jammed a hand through his short hair. This job was a nightmare.

CHAPTER SIX

Sunlight slanted through the closed blinds, and Scarlett stretched on the bed.

"Did you sleep?" Griff said in his deep voice.

Her head whipped to where he was exiting the bathroom. He was fresh out of the shower, and he looked so appealing. She could almost smell his clean scent. Scarlett sucked in air and prayed for strength. "Lord have mercy," she murmured.

Griff's eyebrows lifted. "Sleep?" he asked.

"It was fine, thank you. You?" She was lying. She'd lain awake last night in the hard double bed, listening to his measured breathing in the double bed next to hers. He'd bought them some juice, water bottles, pretzels, and cookies from the lobby before he came back to the Escalade and parked closer to their room. They'd eaten their snack in silence with that tension just growing and growing. Scarlett had slept in her clothes. The need to climb onto his bed and lay her head in the crook of his shoulder grew all night long.

"Horrible," he admitted, brushing his hand at his hair like she'd seen him do so many times. The move about pulled her under. The muscles in his biceps and triceps flexed. He was much more beautiful than any actor she'd starred with.

"Couldn't sleep from wanting me?" she said, then clapped her hand over her mouth. That was why she couldn't sleep and she was projecting her desires onto him, but she liked that he admitted he'd slept badly. Did it have anything to do with her personally, or just because he felt responsible for her and was worried about the job? Or maybe he was used to a better mattress as well.

His lips curved up and his blue eyes lingered on her before he shut his expression down. "Nope," he said. "Just a crappy mattress."

Scarlett let her hopes die once again as she climbed out of the bed. She stretched her arms above her head and heard the sharp intake of breath from him. With a smile, she took her time stretching from side to side, letting her T-shirt slide up on her abdomen. Sneaking a glance at him, she was rewarded to see his mouth slightly open and his eyes filled with hunger.

"Do I have time to shower?" she asked innocently, as if she had no clue how she affected him. It was a shallow satisfaction. He might react to her physically, but it was obvious he didn't love the real her anymore. She stalked up to him and reached past him for the lotion and conditioner he'd left on the counter outside the shower and toilet part of the bathroom. She let her arm brush the side of his. Wow, his smooth skin felt nice.

"S-sure," Griff muttered. He backed away from her and ran into the counter.

Scarlett grinned as she sashayed into the bathroom. It was a small victory, but at least he was struggling a little bit. She was struggling far too much and didn't see the situation improving anytime soon.

Griff praised himself for making it out of that hotel room without forgetting who he'd become, grabbing Scarlett, and kissing her for at least a few hours. His mama had taught him to be tough, and not loving Scarlett was tougher than taking down a drug cartel.

They filled up with gas and drove through Subway for breakfast sandwiches and drinks before heading north again. Thankfully, Scarlett was more subdued this morning. If she tried to tickle him like she had when he'd been driving last night, he'd be sunk. He wasn't the praying type, but he uttered a quick plea to the saints above that Sutton could find and neutralize the threat so this job would be over soon.

He heard Scarlett's breath go slow and even. He glanced over, and his own diaphragm relaxed as he realized she was asleep. He knew she hadn't slept much last night; he'd lain awake and listened to her breathing patterns, tempted over and over again to crawl onto her bed and hold her. He'd never do anything inappropriate. No matter how hardened he was, he loved and respected his mama too much to ever cross lines with any woman. But just to cradle Scarlett in his arms while she slept? That sounded like his version of heaven.

His thoughts stayed in a downward spiral of daydreaming about Scarlett in his arms while he sped up the I-15 corridor. In Nephi, he found a gas station with an outside bathroom.

Scarlett awoke as he pulled up to the gas pump and shut off the Escalade. "Where are we?" she murmured sleepily.

"Nephi."

"That's a weird name."

He smiled. "The people here think he was a prophet." One of Griff's buddies when he'd first joined the Navy had been LDS, and he'd explained a lot about it to Griff.

"Like a prophet ... here today?"

"Yeah, they have one currently, but this Nephi guy lived in America thousands of years ago."

"Cool." She leaned closer to him, obviously interested.

Griff smiled. That was another thing he loved about Scarlett. She was very open to other people's ideas and beliefs. Even though she was strong in her moral compass, she was one of the least judgmental people he'd ever been around.

"And they have a prophet now?" she asked.

"I think so."

She nodded. "I'd like to meet a prophet today. Like John the Baptist just walking around in a suit and a tie. That'd be amazing, wouldn't it?"

Griff's smile lingered. "I'm sure any person on earth would be willing to set up a meeting with *the* Scarlett Lily."

She rolled her eyes and folded her arms across her slender chest. Griff had to force himself to focus on her face. Not that staring at her gorgeous face was much of a hardship on him, especially now that she didn't have any makeup on. "Lucky you, you get to be with me all the time."

"Lucky me," he agreed, his mouth going dry. "I'm going to fill up with gas; then I'll drive you over to the bathroom." He jumped out and shut his door quickly, not waiting for her response. Man, this was a rough job.

There was a cool breeze, which he really appreciated. It helped him wake up and clear his head from longing for Scarlett.

After he filled up, he drove over to the bathroom, blocking the view from the parking lot with the Escalade. He hurried around and got her door. Searching around, he couldn't see anyone who would get a glimpse of Scarlett.

He took her elbow and hurried her to the women's bathroom, cracked the door open, and glanced around. Empty and only a single bathroom. Perfect.

"I don't know if I can walk in there with bare feet," she muttered.

Griff had forgotten about that. He bent down, unlaced his shoes, and slid out of them.

Scarlett came up close and slid her much smaller feet into his shoes. She glanced up at him as if he'd rescued her from the Eiffel Tower. "Thank you, Griff. That was very thoughtful."

He was going to kiss her right here and now, and nobody in the world would blame him for it. She moistened her lips, making his heart pound harder. A chill wind swept over them and she shivered.

The wind helped wake him up to his responsibilities. He stepped back, even though all he wanted to do was hold her close and shelter her from the wind and the world. "I'll be right here."

"Thanks."

He stood outside the door and waited. Not too long passed before he heard water running, and then Scarlett pushed the door open, flicking water from her hands. "No paper towels," she said.

"Why didn't you use the air dryer?"

Her eyes widened. "You know those things spread germs everywhere, right?"

"I didn't know that."

She stared at him. "You know random facts about the religion practiced in this little town, but you don't know that air dryers pull up all the disgustingness of a public bathroom and put it on your hands?"

Griff laughed. "Good thing we complement each other's knowledge."

Her eyes widened, and he wished he could pull the words back. When he and Scarlett had been together, his mama had told him once how Scarlett, or his Jane in those days, was the perfect complement to him. She softened Griff and inspired him in all the right ways. He'd made the mistake of sharing that with Scarlett. Obviously, she hadn't forgotten.

Scarlett walked close to him, and he pulled in a sharp breath. She slid out of his shoes. "I guess you'll need these now."

He smiled and hurried to slip them back on. Straightening, he opened the passenger's side door. "I'll hurry and use the bathroom; then you can choose one of the many drive-throughs for lunch." He was trying to be funny, as there were exactly two fast-food restaurants off this exit.

"I can't get back in that car," she said.

"You can't stay out here all exposed," he insisted. Was he going to have to pick her up and put her in the vehicle? His body heated up just thinking about it.

"Just while you use the restroom. My bum is killing from all this inactivity."

"No way." No way could he think about her bum. "You've got to be secure."

"I could go in the bathroom with you," she said. "I just need to stand up and stretch."

"You're not going in the bathroom with me." He jammed his hand through his hair. "Only the one pair of shoes." He tried to joke off this tension that she created every time they spoke.

She started doing jumping jacks right there between the bathroom doors and the Escalade.

Griff stared at her. She didn't even have any shoes on. "What are you doing?"

"My bum is on fire." She squatted down and shimmied her backside around for a bit, then jumped up into the air. Griff was going to have to pin her down if she didn't stop soon.

"Please stop ..." He wanted to say *moving like that,* but he couldn't, so he settled for "Saying bum."

She squatted low again, reaching her arms up to the sky. "Why?"

"I ..." How could he tell her he couldn't be thinking about her bum? "Just please don't."

She glared up at him, sassier than ever. "Bum!" She jumped into the air again, landed in the squat, and pushed her hips to the right, then the left. "Ah. Feels so good."

That was it. Griff had no choice. He bent down and scooped her off the ground. Straightening, he held her against his chest. "You've got to stop."

Scarlett leaned into him, her lips suddenly within kissing distance. All the oxygen fled his lungs. "Why?" Her green eyes were so clear and appealing that he couldn't think straight.

"Why what?"

"Why do I need to stop?"

"Because." His gaze flickered to her lips.

She ran her hands up his shoulders and around his neck. Griff groaned. He needed to throw her in the Escalade, and quick, but he was frozen in place.

"Because why, Griff?" She moistened her lips.

"You're killing me, Scarlett," he admitted quietly.

Scarlett tugged his head down closer to hers. "Kiss me, Griff."

The words were said so beautifully, so beseechingly, and it was exactly what he wanted to do. Kiss her and never stop. He was too in control of himself to not stop, but just a quick sample of her lips might be enough to satiate him. He leaned closer, and she arched up.

"Oh, excuse me," a woman's voice said from behind them.

Griff cradled Scarlett into his chest, hoping the woman hadn't seen her face. Scarlett buried her face against him, thankfully understanding the danger of someone reporting where they saw her to the world. "My wife isn't feeling well," Griff lied easily, but the thought of Scarlett being his wife made his legs weaken.

"Oh, the poor thing," the lady said.

"Excuse me for just a moment, and I'll get her in the car and we'll get out of your way."

"Of course." The lady stepped back.

Griff loaded Scarlett into the seat, muttering, "Put your head between your legs."

She obeyed.

He shut Scarlett's door and forced a smile at the woman. "Thank you."

She smiled back. "Such a sweet husband," she crooned.

It was all Griff could do not to growl something fierce back at her. He'd never been called sweet by anyone, at least not anyone who wanted to live to talk about it, and he would *never* be a husband. "Thanks," he muttered, and he hurried around the vehicle and jumped into the driver's seat.

"Don't you need to use the bathroom?" Scarlett asked him, tilting her head up from her bent-over position to look at him.

"I'll be fine." Living through SEAL training had toughened him in so many ways, and he could go without sleep, food, or bathroom privileges as long as anybody he knew. If only he could go without Scarlett Lily.

She smiled tremulously up at him. He wondered what had her shaken—the woman almost seeing her face, or the near kiss. His money was on the near kiss. He should be praising the lady for interrupting what would've been a mistake, but he couldn't bring himself to do it. She'd ruined his chance to kiss Scarlett, and that was worse than calling him sweet.

CHAPTER SEVEN

Scarlett seemed fidgety, but she was blessedly quiet through Utah and into Idaho. Griff kept thinking about her "bum on fire" and their near kiss and had to shift his thoughts to something else. He knew she wasn't trying to be difficult, but she was more than difficult for him. He couldn't remain focused when she was so cute and appealing.

"The next Wal-Mart I see, I'll stop and get us food, clothes, toiletries, and shoes for you," he added, forcing a smile.

She simply nodded.

"You've probably never had clothes from a Wal-Mart," he tried to tease, wondering why he was prolonging a conversation with her. It was so much smarter to remain detached and quiet.

"Not since I was a kid," she admitted. "As long as they're warm, I don't care."

He glanced over at her. "Are you cold?"

She nodded again, this time in more of a jerk.

"I apologize. I don't notice change in temperature much." Another bonus of SEAL training torture. "There's dual control; you can turn up the heat as much as you like. There are probably also blankets in the back. "

She messed with the controls, and he could feel heat pouring from her side of the vehicle. He might be sweating in a bit, but he didn't mind. Why hadn't she told him she was cold? He'd been trained to be a gentleman and wanted her to be comfortable.

"So you watch my movies?" she asked suddenly.

"What makes you think that?" That was random for her to bring up, but he knew exactly where she was going and had been waiting for it since last night.

"'You aren't a human lie detector'?" She had him, and judging by the smug look in her eyes, she knew it.

"I saw the last one," he admitted. Griff prided himself on his honesty, but there was no way he'd reveal that he watched every movie, sometimes over and over again. Though he tried to anticipate and fast-forward any kissing parts. Thankfully, she mostly did action shows, and he was very impressed, and grateful, that she refused to do love scenes.

"What did you think?" she asked quietly.

Griff had to look at her. She sounded like she needed his approval or something. That was insane. She was Scarlett Lily, famous A-list actress. When her gaze met his, he felt electrified and drawn to her. The vulnerability in her eyes told him she wasn't full of herself like he'd tried to make himself believe all these years. It had been a way to keep his distance, convincing himself she had men all over her and she'd become an overconfident diva. Being around her, he knew he'd deluded himself, at least about the diva part.

"You're ... very good," he admitted. She was much more than "very good," but he didn't want to come across as gushing. He cleared his throat and focused on the road. "Why don't you make me a list of what you will need for the next couple of weeks—clothes, your shoe size, food you like, toiletries, stuff like that."

"Okay."

"There should be a pen and something to write on in the glove box."

She rummaged around and found a pen and pad of paper. She started writing the list as he cruised through southern Idaho. She wrote and wrote and wrote. Griff was already sweating from the heat pouring out of her vents, and the length of the list had him sweating more.

"I can't haul the entire store to Island Park," he said.

She glanced up at him. "I'm just writing down the basics."

His eyebrows went up. "I forgot that you're a princess." It was said semi-teasingly.

"And I forgot that you're a jerk."

Griff smiled and relaxed. It would be much better the next few weeks of being stuck alone with her if she thought he was a jerk. Most people did, and it was an easy role for him to play.

"I should be grateful that lady interrupted back in Nephi and you didn't kiss me," she said. "Would you have kissed me, Griff?"

Sweat rolled down his back as he had no clue what to say. Dang straight he would've. She'd just called him a jerk. Maybe she'd realized what a huge mistake she'd be making by kissing him. Griff was pretty sure it was divine intervention when he saw a Wal-Mart off the right exit. Maybe praying did help. He darted through two lanes of traffic. Scarlett let out a little squeal as he flew down the exit ramp.

"Sorry," he muttered. Sorry that he couldn't talk to her and sorry that he'd scared her, but mostly sorry that he couldn't kiss her like he wanted to.

"Maybe you'll kill me with your driving before I can get kidnapped."

He knew the words were meant to be teasing, but his stomach churned at the very thought of her kidnapper taking her. He'd seen horrors that would make his mama sob and had sadly become hardened to the constant heartache, but imagining Scarlett in some scumball's grasp made his stomach churn and his palms sweat until he had trouble gripping the steering wheel.

He pulled into the Wal-Mart parking lot and slammed it into park. He held out his hand. "I'll be quick."

"You're going to make me sit here?" She didn't hand over the paper. "Sore *bum* and all?"

Griff let himself look at her. She was so appealing to him, he didn't know if he was strong enough to tell her no to any request she might make. He heard those words bounce around in his head again: *Kiss me, Griff.* He hoped she wouldn't make that irresistible plea a second time or he would cave.

He took a more pragmatic approach. "If you waltz into Wal-Mart in Idaho Falls, an hour from our destination, people are going to be taking pictures, posting them on Instagram, and you will be putting yourself in danger." The vultures that would be pursuing her for the million-dollar paycheck would converge on any place where she'd been sighted, searching under every rock and backwoods cabin. So far nothing had leaked from their encounter in St. George, but that was seven hours south of here.

She nodded tightly and shifted in her seat.

Griff hated for her to be uncomfortable. He glanced around the Escalade. "If I put the seats down, would you want to stretch out in the back?" That would accomplish a couple purposes: she'd be able to change her position, and he could keep wandering eyes from looking in the front windshield and spotting her like that guy had done last night. The rear windows in the Escalade were not only bulletproof; they were impossible to see through.

"Okay." She handed over her list. Griff shoved it in his pocket, hurried around to put down the seats, and then waited until she'd crawled into the back and covered up with a blanket before muttering goodbye and locking her in.

He rushed into the store and pulled out her list. It was longer than Scarlett's long red hair. Clothes, toiletries, food, she'd listed multiple items under each category, most of the time with specific brands. He blew out a breath and headed for the women's clothing first, suspecting she was laughing to herself in the Escalade. He'd play her game and buy everything on the list, but he was going to get her back, somehow.

CHAPTER EIGHT

Scarlett stretched out in the back of the Escalade. The fleece blanket kept her warm enough. She wondered if Griff would just trash the list and buy what he wanted. She wouldn't put it past him. As long as she got some warm clothes and shoes, she'd deal without the rest of the items on her list.

She needed to use a restroom again, but she understood why Griff didn't want anyone to see her. Most Americans would recognize her on sight, and the people pursuing her would take notice if she was spotted this close to the place where Griff was taking her to hide. The thought made her stomach tighten with fear. She knew Griff could best any man or woman, but if they came in hordes hoping to make a million dollars, he might be overrun.

She had almost fallen asleep when the back door opened and Griff's handsome face peeked in. "Stay there," he whispered, tilting his head to the right. Another customer must be close by, putting their own groceries in the car. She scooted to the side, and he started piling bag after bag into the rear of the Escalade. He'd bought plenty. Maybe he had used her list.

She rummaged in the bag closest to her and found translucent face powder, night cream, tinted moisturizer, eyeliner, and lip stain. She smiled. They were the brands she used to use back in high school and college, not her high-dollar makeup of today. You couldn't find her current brands at Wal-Mart, and it was really sweet of Griff to follow her list so closely. Luckily she had eyelash extensions, so she didn't have to mess with mascara. She pulled out a bottle of hair dye—golden blonde. "What is this?"

Griff unloaded another armful of bags and focused on her. His blue eyes glinted and his lips turned up in a smirk. "Thought it might be smart to change your look."

"Smart ... or are we taking a trip down memory lane?" She folded her arms across her chest and narrowed her eyes at him. Did Griff prefer her as a blonde? It was her natural color, but her agent had suggested red when she started acting. The vibrant color stood out from the many blondes and brunettes, securing her roles she didn't think she would've gotten. Red had become a trademark for her.

Griff simply smiled, unloaded the last of the bags, and slammed the rear door shut. Ooh, that man could infuriate her. She scrambled back to the front of the vehicle. He climbed into the driver's seat. Scarlett climbed over the console, her skirt sliding up, and she heard Griff groan. She froze, wondering what was wrong. Glancing over at him, she saw he was focused on her legs.

His eyes traveled up her legs and body until they rested on her smiling face. He glowered at her. "Do you need help?" he gritted out.

"I would appreciate that, kind sir."

Griff's jaw tightened, and then he moved so quickly she had no time to react. He wrapped his arms around her waist and pulled her upper body closer to him; she assumed it was an attempt to straighten her legs out so she could slide into her seat. But he froze when her face came within inches of his. His breath quickened, and when she saw he was staring at her mouth, she was soon panting for air as well.

A horn beeped somewhere in the parking lot. Griff's eyes opened wider. He released his grip on her waist and muttered gruffly, "We'd better go."

Scarlett nodded, feeling shell-shocked. She slid into her seat and fastened the seat belt. As they drove out of Idaho Falls, she kept casting glances at him, but he was studiously focused on the road. Scarlett sighed and crossed her legs, which earned her a quick dart of his eyes before he turned forward again. She needed a restroom, but she needed Griff to kiss her even more.

CHAPTER NINE

They left the freeway and drove through some snow-covered farmland before hitting the forested area of Island Park. The snow got deeper amongst the trees, but thankfully the roads were clear. Even with the heat blowing on high and the fleece blanket from the back, she shivered seeing all of that snow, and because she needed the restroom even more now.

Scarlett endured her discomfort in silence, giving up on Griff talking to her, or even looking at her. Another near kiss and he appeared to have shut down completely. He'd claimed Idaho Falls was only an hour from Island Park, but apparently he had meant the area, not the place where they were actually staying.

Dusk was falling as he finally pulled off the main road and stopped at an imposing gate with a serious fence extending in both directions. The sight of that gate and fence, and the security they intended to provide, helped Scarlett's worries ease. The tougher-than-anyone Griff Quinn could protect her, but it was nice to know that nobody was getting through that gate without some serious equipment.

Griff punched in a code, and then a screen came up on the gate. He leaned out the window. She could hear him talking to someone on the screen. It was impressive security, but she was honestly going to have an accident on the leather seat if he didn't hurry.

Finally, the gate swung open and they eased through. They drove along an asphalt driveway for what seemed like many miles, although it was probably only one.

They eased into a clearing in the trees where a massive three-story log cabin dominated the scene, glowing with multiple exterior lights. "Cabin" didn't quite fit; it was more of a mansion. She wished she could see more of the area around it, but the darkness was encroaching.

"Wow," she murmured.

"It's a nice place," Griff said.

He drove around the side of the house and down a gradual slope to a basement garage entry—an entry with five large doors. She wondered who his friends were. Many of Griff's family members were ultra-wealthy, so this might be one of their homes, but he'd said this belonged to a friend.

Griff jumped out and typed in a code on the panel. One of the garage doors slid open and automatic lights lit the interior. Griff climbed back in, pulled into the garage, and shut off the vehicle. There were only some four-wheelers, snowmobiles, a side-by-side, and a Jeep in the huge garage space.

Griff glanced over at her as she shifted in her seat. "You okay?"

"I want to get out, but I'm afraid I'll ... pee my pants."

He shook his head. "Wait, then." He popped out of his door, hurried around to hers, and swung it open.

Scarlett started to ease her legs out, but Griff slid his warm hands under her legs and upper back and lifted her from the vehicle. Scarlett's breath rushed out at his nearness, and she almost forgot how badly she needed a restroom.

Griff glanced down at her. "Figured this might help you not 'pee your pants'." He actually smiled at her.

Scarlett wrapped her arms around his neck, and now he was the one with the breath rushing out in a pop. "Hmm. You sure it wasn't because you want me close?"

His grin disappeared and he hurried through the garage, pushing the handle and then the door open into the house. He went down a hallway softly lit by built-in night lights, past a large room on the left. From what she could see, and from the familiar rubbery smell, the room housed a bunch of fitness equipment.

Griff stopped next to a closed door and released the hand holding her legs. She slid to her feet, but she stayed close to him with his hand lingering on her back and her arms around his neck. The moment slowed down and went sticky between them. Scarlett released her clasp on his neck and slowly trailed her fingers along his broad shoulders. Griff wrapped both hands around her hips and pulled her in tight to his chest.

Scarlett's breath quickened, and she pushed herself up onto her tiptoes. She was still a few inches from his lips, though. He had to help out, bend down a little bit, act like he wanted to kiss her. Was it really so hard for him to react appropriately?

Griff didn't move. He stared at her and stared at her. Scarlett loved his blue gaze focused on her, but she could wait no longer.

"Goodness," she huffed out. "I really have to pee."

Griff released her, pushed the door open behind her, and stepped back. "Don't let me keep you."

"Ugh!" Scarlett hurried into the bathroom, seething with frustration and an ache that only Griff could fill. She used the bathroom, replaying in her mind how many times that man had almost kissed her. What was he waiting for? It was true that not all of the near misses had been his fault, like the lady interrupting them outside the bathroom in Nephi, but she feared that given the choice, Griff wouldn't kiss her. His prized self-control would never slip. How did she convince him he needed to kiss her? Even more important, how did she convince him he needed her?

She washed her hands and studied herself in the mirror. She looked tired and disheveled. Her eyeliner and lipstick were gone, and she could really use some translucent powder on her nose and forehead. The entire long drive here seemed like a blur now.

There was another question she had to ask herself. Was it smart to keep growing closer to Griff Quinn? He'd broken her heart ten years ago, and he didn't appear to have any regrets for doing so. Why would she willingly put herself in his arms and let him tear her apart all over again?

Griff put his head down and worked, refusing to talk to or even look at Scarlett as they unloaded the Escalade. She was diligent, trying to help, but he could carry ten bags to her four. They got all the food to the open kitchen area on the main level and into the fridge, freezer, and pantry; then they unloaded the clothes and toiletries from the back of the Escalade. He grabbed his duffel bag, that Sutton or Jasmine had thought to put in, and gestured for her to go in front of him on the stairs. They ascended to the main level, and when she hesitated there, he grunted. "Up one more."

The suites were all on the second level, with the exception of Tucker and Maryn's master suite, which took up the entire third level. Griff rarely went up there when he'd been here to go on hunts or snowmobile rides with his buddies Tucker and Cal Johnson, great men he knew from military ops long ago.

He made the mistake of focusing on Scarlett's slender form as she ascended the stairs in front of him. The memory of her in his arms rushed over him. Why did she have to be so appealing? He couldn't even remember half of the women who had tried to pursue him throughout the years. Saying no had never been a problem for him. He had a higher calling to save lives and protect the innocent, as well as protect any woman from having a relationship with the likes of him. A beautiful woman couldn't dissuade him from that. But he'd been lying to himself. Scarlett could yank all his lofty ideals out from under him and have him begging at her feet like a puppy, hoping for one simple pat on his head.

He shook his head as they reached the second story. No. He was Griff Quinn. He was stronger than the memories of what he'd had with Scarlett and the pull he felt toward her now. He couldn't succumb to her sweet smile, her teasing voice, or her clear green eyes. Saying it wasn't fair for her to be with someone like him was so inadequate that he didn't waste time going there.

Scarlett looked over her shoulder at him with those beguiling eyes. In the dimly lit hallway, without the usual makeup and fancy clothing he'd gotten used to seeing her in when he Googled her, she looked so soft and appealing. He tripped over nothing and almost went down. Scarlett dropped her bags and reached out to steady him. Her soft fingers wrapped around his forearm.

Griff pulled back quickly, embarrassed at his awkwardness and even more embarrassed at the way he was reacting to her. He could battle several men at once and not falter, and he'd just tripped over this beautiful woman. Ridiculous. *Get in control*, he told himself.

He gestured toward the first open door. "This okay?"

She shrugged. "Sure." Picking her bags up, she walked into the room with him right at her heels.

Griff flipped on the light with his elbow. This entire level was suites for guests. He thought there were seven or eight suites, but he couldn't remember for sure. When he'd gotten hold of Tucker, his friend had told him he'd have the housekeepers come through the house, and then he'd remotely get the lights and heat on. He asked if Griff wanted him to have the fridge stocked with fresh food, but Griff felt like his friend was doing more than enough and had declined.

He followed Scarlett through the room and into the attached bathroom and closet. Setting down all of the bags that contained the junk she'd had on that list, he clung to his bag of essentials and backed away.

"Good night," he said, turning away before he had to torture himself with her beautiful face any longer tonight. At least they were finally here and not stuck in the Escalade together. He had to smile as he remembered her tickling him last night, but the smile faded quickly as he thought of how many times he'd almost kissed her. He was stronger than that, or at least he used to be. Yet what mere mortal could be strong when Scarlett Lily was smiling at them?

"Aren't you hungry?" Scarlett asked.

Griff stopped but didn't turn around. "Too tired," he lied. He *was* tired, but their drive-through lunch hadn't been enough and his stomach was eating itself at this point. Didn't matter. He'd hide out in his suite until he was sure she was asleep; then he'd go grab something in the kitchen. "Feel free to eat whatever you like, though."

With that, he hurried from the room, down the hallway, and into the suite next door. He wouldn't let himself think about what compelled him to pick this suite. He was supposed to protect Scarlett; that meant being close by, right? He shut the bedroom door, dropped the bags in the closet, stripped off his clothes, and started the shower, turning the handle to cold. He was tired, hungry, and completely irrational where Scarlett was concerned. Staying far away from her was as important right now as protecting her.

CHAPTER TEN

Scarlett heard the shower start, and her stomach did a dance before it settled. Griff was so close, yet as unattainable as if he were still deployed. She started to unload the toiletries and makeup in the shower and drawers, noticing that the basics like shampoo, conditioner, lotion, and toothpaste were already in the bathroom. There was also some face wash and day and night cream in the cabinets. Those were all closer to the brands she usually had her shopping consultant purchase. Whoever owned this house was generous and thoughtful.

When she pulled out peaches-and-cream shampoo, conditioner, body wash, and lotion from the supplies Griff had bought, her eyes widened. She hadn't requested any of this. It was the very brand and scent she'd used in college, when she didn't have any money for expensive perfume. Griff had always told her back then how much he loved the way she smelled. Hmm. Maybe the gruff Griff Quinn wasn't as impervious to her as she thought.

Stacking the clothes Griff had purchased for her in the closet, she couldn't resist sliding a soft sweatshirt over her T-shirt, pulling her skirt off and putting on some leggings, and slipping on some warm socks. The house was nice and warm, but all that snow outside ... She shuddered just thinking about it.

Griff's shower was still running when she padded out into the hallway. She made her way downstairs and ate a cheese stick, some carrots, and a handful of almonds. Not a fabulous dinner, but she didn't feel like cooking right now. She wandered around the main area and stopped in front of a display of wedding photos on the mantel; she recognized the couple as Tucker and Maryn Shaffer. Tucker was a brilliant billionaire who had invented the Friend Zone, a social media site that surpassed all the rest. He was almost as big as Griff's brother Mack, and he looked imposing with dark hair and serious eyes. His wife was a petite blonde whose smile and bright blue eyes lit up the room. Scarlett had met them both at a party and thought they were great. So these were Griff's friends. Good friends to have.

She should've gone back up to her room, but she didn't want to listen to Griff's shower running. Instead, she flicked the gas fireplace on and padded over to the couch. Pulling a blanket over her, she stared into the flames for a while. She wondered why Griff had to be so strong and distant. Every chance they got to connect was ruined somehow, mostly by him.

Footsteps came on the stairs. Scarlett stood, letting the blanket drop onto the couch and turning toward the entrance to the great room.

Griff strode in, headed for the kitchen. When he saw her, he came up short. "I thought you were asleep," he said too quickly, as if he was nervous to be around her.

"Nope." She was getting really tired of his games.

"Maybe you should get some rest. It's been a long couple of days."

"You're the one who drove the entire time. I bet you're exhausted."

He simply nodded, but he did look tired. He looked incredible, too; he'd come fresh out of the shower, so his dark blond hair was even darker than normal.

"Sit down and I'll make you something to eat," she offered. He'd upended his life to protect her. She knew it was what he did, but she also knew this assignment couldn't be any easier on him than it was on her, especially with the way he acted like he didn't want to be with her. It hurt, but she still appreciated that he'd take the job and be here for her when it was hard.

"No, thank you. I'll get something tomorrow."

"Sit down," she commanded, pointing to the high-back barstools lining the long granite island.

His eyebrows jumped, but he didn't comply.

Scarlett marched around the couch and kept coming until she was right in his space. He smelled so clean and good, but she couldn't let that distract her. "Look, I know this isn't easy for you, but we're going to be stuck here for who knows how long.

We might as well get comfortable and enjoy each other's company."

Griff's blue gaze was wary as he blinked down at her. "I don't think that's a good idea, Scarlett."

"Come on, Griff." She groaned and reached out a hand to him. "We were good friends once. We're adults. I think we can put the heartache behind us and be friends again."

His eyes went from her face down to her outstretched hand, then back up again, several times. Scarlett tried to wait patiently. She wanted so much more than friendship from Griff, but it was becoming all too clear she wasn't going to get it. They could at least try to be comfortable around each other the next few weeks, stuck in this gorgeous mansion.

Griff clasped his hands behind his back, shook his head, and took a large step back. "I really need some space right now," he pushed out. Then he pivoted and all but fled out of the great room. She heard his footsteps pound up the steps and then his door shut.

Scarlett stood there, stunned. He needed space? Her hands shook with frustration. She'd give him space, then, the jerk.

She clicked off the fire and went to her own room. Saying a quick prayer of gratitude for being safe, and even thanking her Father in heaven for Griff being the one protecting her, she begged the Lord to show her His purpose here. Right now nothing made sense to her, especially her ache for Griff and his obvious refusal to be near her.

CHAPTER ELEVEN

Scarlett slept better thanks to a high-quality mattress and the fact that she was completely exhausted. When she awoke, the sun was blinding off the mounds of snow outside. She wondered if Griff had slept and where he was. Standing and stretching, she padded into the bathroom, searched through the clothes Griff had bought her, and put on a T-shirt, shorts, socks, and some no-name running shoes. If only she could run outside. She looked out there and shivered. Not happening.

Exiting her room, she strained to hear movement that would indicate where Griff was, but nothing came. She walked down the stairs, detouring to the large living area and grabbing a water bottle from the kitchen before going back to the entryway and taking the steps downstairs. The sounds of weights clanking drifted from the workout room, and she smiled. Griff needed space? She'd see if he really wanted it.

She pushed open the workout room door and had to lean against the doorframe. Griff was wearing a fitted T-shirt and shorts and performing a lateral raise. The muscles in his shoulders and arms were all engaged, his skin glowed from a slight polish of sweat, and he was completely glorious to behold.

He caught her gaze in the full-length mirrors and lowered the weights to the racks before turning to face her. "Hey."

She smiled. "Good morning. Care if I share the gym?"

He swallowed and shook his head slightly. "Of course not."

Scarlett headed for the treadmill to warm up. The gym was small, and she liked the intimacy of exercising near Griff. They used to lift together in college all the time.

She started at a walk and quickly broke into a jog. Glancing away from the panel, she caught Griff staring at her. He didn't glance away, and that made her irrationally happy. She smiled at him, remembering long runs in the California sun with him. "Do you still like to run?"

Griff nodded, picked up some huge dumbbells, and started into bicep curls. "Yeah, but I hate the treadmill."

"Really?" Scarlett tried to talk normally, but her mouth was watering at the vision of his well-defined biceps as he lifted and lowered the weights. "At home I have my Kindle and I can jog for hours while I read."

"Wow. I'd probably get dizzy and fall off the back."

Scarlett maintained a steady jog, excited they were having a normal conversation. Maybe she could convince him they could be friends again, and maybe a miracle would happen and they'd get past friends. "You're like the ultra-athlete. I'm sure you could run blindfolded."

"Thanks." He re-shelved the weights and turned to her, folding his arms across his chest. "You're ... really fit." He swallowed again, and she had to hide a smile. "Do you have trainers work with you?"

"Almost every day." She wondered what everyone at home was thinking. She'd heard Griff tell his sister-in-law to get a hold of her parents, and that was all she really cared about.

"Impressive," he muttered. He hurried as far away from her as he could and started using the cable machine for reverse flies.

Scarlett had nothing to stare at but him. It was more fun to watch him work out than any reading material she might have used to pass the time. A few times he caught her watching him. He didn't maintain eye contact, and that was disappointing. She'd love some long, searching gazes from him. He could teach any action hero how to look and fight, but he failed miserably as a romantic interest. Too bad for her that he was the only romantic interest she wanted.

Forcing herself to increase her speed, she ran at a faster pace but was still able to watch Griff almost uninterrupted.

He set down a barbell he was using for overhead presses, whirled on her, and pinned her with a frustrated look. "Why are you staring at me?"

Scarlett arched her eyebrows. "I don't have anything to read."

He pushed out a breath and muttered, "Just a second." Hurrying through the door, he disappeared.

Scarlett upped her speed and did a long sprint until she heard his footsteps returning. She slowed to a walk as he strode back in with a handful of magazines. Scarlett stopped the treadmill as he approached. She got a whiff of his clean, masculine scent and hoped she smelled good. If she was lucky the peaches-and-cream lotion would drive him crazy.

Griff handed over the magazines, and their hands brushed. Warmth rushed through her. Could he feel the connection as strongly as she did? The depth of his blue gaze said he did. "These were the only magazines I could find," he said. "There are a bunch of books in the office on the main level, but I didn't know if they'd stay open while you ran."

"Thank you." She forced herself to look at the magazine covers. *The Rising Star*. She was on the cover of one of them with B.C. Knight. They'd done an article about one of her recent movies, *The Fearless Warrior*. She glanced back up at Griff and held up the magazine. "Weird to read about yourself."

"I bet. What's B.C. Knight like?"

"He's an amazing guy."

Griff grunted, and his eyes flashed with a predatory gleam. Scarlett felt something stir in her abdomen. He was jealous. Didn't he know B.C. was happily married? The fact that Griff felt possessive of her for any reason made her hot all over.

Scarlett set the magazines on the treadmill holder and stepped off and close to him. "Does that bother you?"

"Why would it bother me?" he threw back at her, but he didn't step away.

Scarlett lifted her shoulders. "I don't know. Maybe part of you still cares."

Griff stared at her and pushed out a ragged breath. Neither of them moved, and Scarlett prayed he'd admit to feeling something for her. He broke eye contact and rushed for the door, muttering, "I need to check the security cameras." Then he was gone.

Scarlett deflated against the treadmill. This man was harder to get through to than a rhinoceros. He had a thicker skin than one, too. Dang Griff Quinn all the way to purgatory. She still loved him, and he couldn't even admit that he cared about her. She returned to the treadmill and pushed the speed and incline up. Working out hard might keep her from crying over what they'd lost. Heaven knew she'd gone to that miserable place far too many times over the years.

Griff had never felt like a wimp before, but he did right now. He'd literally run from the workout room, muttering some excuse, to escape telling Scarlett how impressive she was, how much he still cared. He had to be more vigilant than this. He could not allow himself to interact casually with her.

The security devices were top notch, and there were cameras in all the main areas of the house and the hallways and stairwells.

He'd simply carry a device everywhere and monitor Scarlett and the property that way. He could avoid her and keep his sanity.

If only he could keep himself from remembering how amazing it felt to hold her in his arms. No! He couldn't be thinking thoughts like that. He was on a job. Scarlett was an assignment. Feelings could not factor in. Romance, love, and an irresistible woman were not on his radar. Somehow he'd stay detached and strong until they found the man who'd put the bounty on Scarlett's head.

He hurried for his shower, frustrated that he hadn't made it through his workout and more frustrated that he had to stay away from the fabulous woman sharing this mansion with him. He might need to pray for strength. Sadly, prayer had never worked out for him.

CHAPTER TWELVE

The next few days puttered by slower than any days Scarlett could remember. Even when she wasn't on a tight schedule with a movie in production, she was busy catching up, dealing with sponsors, her agent, her tax or investment people, dress designers, image consultants, personal trainers, or a hundred other things that needed to be caught up on. Now she was stuck in a mansion in Island Park with nothing to do but exercise, read, watch movies, and cook elaborate meals because she was so bored, and it was wearing on her. The world outside was covered in ice and snow. It was picturesque with a slow-moving river easing through the backyard and loads of pine trees loaded down with white fluff, but she didn't have the gear to go out and explore the winter wonderland.

Griff had gotten almost everything on her list at Wal-Mart and even more warm clothes than she'd asked for, but she didn't have a coat or boots that would fit her. She'd even searched through Maryn and Tucker's lockers in the mudroom, but everything of Maryn's was miniscule and everything's of Tucker's was huge.

Griff had made himself impressively scarce the last three days. The house was big, but it wasn't that big. He was obviously avoiding her and working hard to do it. If they ran into each other, he'd give her a forced smile, murmur some excuse, and hurry away. She'd seen him outside her bedroom windows a few times, but she couldn't see that he was doing anything out in the snow besides pacing around. She knew he spent hours in the home gym, but if she put on some of the workout gear he'd thoughtfully bought for her and walked in, he'd leave quickly. She cooked dinner every night, by herself, and left it out on the counter. Hours later, she'd check and see that the food had been eaten and everything was cleaned up. Yet he never ate with her or even thanked her. He really was a jerk.

The constant rejection hurt. Wasn't it enough that he'd rejected her back in their college days? Did he have to keep repeating the action, make sure she knew not even to dream about him?

He had sought her out earlier today and told her he'd heard from Sutton and they had some leads. They should find the person who instigated her hit soon. Griff had looked relieved that this job might be over. She should be too. She didn't want to be stuck here much longer, but any hope she had of a breakthrough with Griff would disappear when she went back home. Ten long years of wishing he'd reappear, and then when he did, nothing came of it. Nobody would watch a movie this depressing. If she turned it into a movie, she'd have Griff kissing her every chance he got, multiple bad guys appearing, and the two of them running for their lives, while holding on to each other's hands, of course.

She sighed as she scrubbed her face and got ready for bed. She should be happy their existence was mundane. It meant she was safe, but couldn't she be safe and in Griff's arms? She heard his door open and close next door. She'd found that interesting. Seven suites on this floor, and he'd chosen the one right next door to hers. Probably just for safety reasons. Their balconies even connected, not that she could even get that door open with the mounds of snow on the patio. Snow in March. No matter how pretty it was here, she wouldn't choose to have a home in a cold location like this. She preferred beaches and sunny skies.

Picking up the bottle of blonde hair dye that she'd left out on the counter, she turned it over in her hands. Why had Griff truly bought it? They were hidden here; she didn't need some disguise. Maybe he preferred her as a blonde. The thought that he preferred her at all made her stomach warm. She rolled her eyes and set the bottle down. Her hair stylist would ream her if she used cheap bleach like this on her long, thick, hair. It would probably damage it and she'd have to cut it off. Her agent and image consultants would have lots to say about that. Well, they weren't stuck in a remote cabin with the only man they'd ever loved and completely losing their minds, now, were they?

Scarlett finally lay down in the bed, stretching out under the warm blankets. Everything about this home was comfortable and luxurious, but it wasn't any fun being here basically by herself. She could only imagine how happy Maryn and Tucker Shaffer would be here, but few people had beautiful relationships like those two. Scarlett certainly didn't, probably never would.

She tossed and turned, trying to find a position where she would sleep. The longer she lay awake, the more frustrated she became. She wanted to run into the suite next door, pound on Griff's chest, and demand he tell her why he'd left her all those years ago. Didn't she deserve an explanation? She knew he'd loved her in college. That love was so far gone, and she didn't know why she couldn't just let it all go.

Men throughout the world would give anything for a single date with her. She didn't let it make her overconfident, because she understood that they didn't know the real her. Why did the only man she'd ever wanted want nothing to do with her? It must be a reflection on her, then, because Griff truly knew her and he'd left without looking back.

She'd dated a lot of impressive men but had never found anyone like Griff. It was interesting that she always chose to date the tough guy. Her latest boyfriend was Josh Porter, the NHL hockey star. He was a great guy, tough, and a lot like Griff in that he didn't waste words and he had impeccable manners. Yet it hadn't hurt her at all when Josh had reconnected with the love of his youth, Hannah Hall. Scarlett had been happy for both of them and only wondered why she couldn't connect with the love of her youth.

She gritted her teeth and rolled over, punching the pillow. Reality wasn't enjoyable. She'd make sure to never say yes to an unrequited love story. She was also done with rom-coms and dramas. Action or suspense movies were her focus from here on out.

"Jane!" The scream from Griff's room was loud enough to make her ears ring.

She froze under the covers. Griff would only yell like that, and yell her real name, if someone had broken into their sanctuary. Should she run to him, or stay hidden? Was it a warning yell, or a *come to me so I can protect you* yell?

She waited for a few seconds, then decided to move. He wouldn't yell like that if he wanted her to hide.

Scrambling out of the covers, she ran to her bedroom door, her hand trembling as she pushed the lever handle down and pulled the door toward her. She searched the hallway, which was dimly lit with the built-in night lights. She couldn't hear or see anything. Cold sweat pricked at her neck as she crept into the hallway. She was so grateful now that Griff had chosen the bedroom next to hers. She just wanted him close, wanted to know he would protect her.

"Jane! No!" Griff yelled.

Scarlett jumped, screamed, and sprinted for his door. Pushing down the handle, she flung it open, slammed it closed, and then ran for him.

Griff sat up in bed. The half moon reflecting off the snow outside gave her enough light to see his chest, arms, and face. His well-defined chest and arms looked so safe and inviting. His face scrunched with confusion. "Scarlett?" he asked, reverting to her actress name now he was awake.

Scarlett ran to him, diving against him and knocking him back to his pillows. His arms instinctively wrapped around her. She burrowed her head in his chest. "Do we need to move? Who did you see? Are you okay?" She rapid-fired the questions at him.

"What?" He sounded disoriented and unsure, which was so unlike Griff. He pushed her away from him and slipped out of the covers, his eyes darting around the room. "Did you hear something?" He grabbed a device off the nightstand and peered at it. "Nothing from the security cameras."

Scarlett stood, feeling shaky. "No, it was you. You were screaming my name."

He whirled on her. "You didn't see someone?"

"No. I was lying there and I heard you scream my name, so I came to you."

His blue eyes searched over her carefully. Finally, he nodded. "Sometimes I have nightmares. I apologize if I scared you. Just to be safe, I'll come check your room, and then you can get some rest while I check the rest of the house."

Scarlett folded her arms across her chest. His words were all formal and detached, but she could see deep in his eyes that he wasn't impervious to worrying about her. It emboldened her to say, "So you sometimes have nightmares ..." She paused, and he gave her a slight bob of his head. "Where you scream *my* name?"

She had him, and they both knew it. His eyes flashed with warmth for her and he took a step closer. Scarlett was such a sucker for him that she almost ran headlong into his broad chest.

The military shutter went over his face quickly. Scarlett blinked, and the man who cared for her was gone. "Stay close to me while I check your room," he muttered, walking to the door and swinging it partway open. He glanced around the hallway, listening. She concentrated on his back; the skin there looked bumpy, but she couldn't see it clearly in the darkened room. After a tense moment, Griff looked over his shoulder at her and motioned with his head.

Scarlett rolled her eyes. She was so fed up with him right now. This scene would've been the perfect opportunity for him to notice how afraid she was, cuddle her close, and admit that he yelled her name in his sleep because he'd never let her go from his heart. But no, not Griff. He stayed all strong and detached. He'd die alone rather than admit he cared for her. Sadly for her, that meant she'd die alone too. Why couldn't she get over him?

"Come on." He gestured with his hand.

"No. It was just your nightmare; there's no one here. And I would like to discuss why you scream my name in your sleep."

Griff slowly walked back to her. His gaze was cold and quite honestly terrifying. The sheer power of his build would have many people cowering. Scarlett simply glared at him. She knew he'd never hurt her, and he was going to have to pick her up and throw her in her bedroom to get her out of his.

"I need you to cooperate with me, Jane, or I can't guarantee your safety."

"Maybe I don't want to be safe." She jutted out her chin.

"That is the stupidest thing you've ever said. You want to be kidnapped and taken to some man who would pay a million dollars to rape you?"

Scarlett recoiled at that horrible word, but she wasn't backing down with him. "Ask me what I really want, Griff."

He stared at her, grunting in disgust. "No."

Scarlett shut her eyes, then opened them and tried to beg him with her gaze. It was too dark to see clearly, but between the moon and the night lights, she thought he could guess her intentions. She stepped closer to him, inhaled his clean scent, and poked him in that solid and inviting chest. "Ask me."

He wrapped his hand around hers and she was pretty certain he was going to fling her hand away, but instead he kept it cradled in his palm, close to his heart. Scarlett lifted her other hand and rested it on his nicely formed bicep. Griff let out a soft moan, and her heart lifted—she knew he wasn't impervious to her.

"Please ask me," she murmured. "You stubborn jerk, *please* ask me."

Griff granted her a slight smile. He released her hand and cupped her cheek with his palm. "What do you want, Jane?" he asked in a deep voice that pierced clear through her.

"You." She didn't dare move or hardly even breathe as she studied his face.

His blue eyes darkened to midnight. "Why would you want me?" His voice sounded pained, broken.

"It's always been you, Griff. Always. I never stopped loving you." She'd laid it out there now, and there was no taking it back.

He searched her face for a few beats and she thought maybe he would soften, would admit he loved her too. Then he shook his head. "No. You're wrong to believe you love me. You live in a make-believe world. You don't want me; you want the image of me. The alpha male. The hero. I'm not Hollywood, Scarlett."

Scarlett's heart felt like it was being pummeled by a sledgehammer. She wanted to call him so many names and then cry herself to sleep, but she loved him. Despite her rational brain trying to tell her to wise up and get away, she still loved him.

She should give up now, but she hadn't reached her level of acclaim by doing things halfway. She wrapped both hands around his upper back, prepared to pull herself close and kiss him, show him how much she loved him, and see if she could break through his barriers. Her hands met ridged scars, deep and uneven scars. Scarlett gasped, released him, and moved to go behind him and see what had happened to his perfect back.

Griff wrapped her up tightly in his arms, pinning her against his chest to stop her from moving at all. "Don't," he warned.

"Griff." Scarlett's voice came out in a whimper. She knew what she'd felt. He'd been burned, or whipped, or tortured. All the horrific things that had happened in movies she'd starred in played through her mind, but those weren't real. This was very real, and it had happened to the man she loved.

"It's okay," Griff said in the softest voice she'd heard from him in the past three days. "I'm okay, Jane."

"Is it your entire back?" she whispered, trembling. Who had done that to him?

He nodded, not saying anything more. Her arms were trapped tight to her sides as he kept her in a very firm embrace.

"Let me go, Griff," she said. It was ironic that she'd been begging him to hold her, but now she wanted to be free.

"No."

She would've loved that refusal in any other circumstance. But she needed to see. She needed to kiss his scars and see them for herself, see what had happened to this man she cared so deeply for. "Please, Griff."

"I don't want you to see them."

She looked up at him, his chiseled face outlined by the moonlight. "Who did that to you?"

Griff shook his head and held her more tightly. "Let's get you to bed." Walking with her held tightly against him was awkward. They made it into her room and next to her bed. He released her and gestured with his hand. "Get some rest."

Scarlett shook her head, biting at her lower lip. "I can't sleep thinking that someone tortured you or something." She perversely wanted to see his back, but as much as he didn't want her to see it, she tried to respect him for that.

Griff sighed heavily. "I don't talk about stuff like this with anyone."

"You used to tell me everything."

He studied her and finally admitted, "Yeah, I did."

"What happened to you?" she asked. She meant everything—the scars, the way he'd shut himself off from her, his need to be a hero, and his determination not to let anyone so much as thank him for it.

He studied the bed, his arms folded tightly across his chest. The muscles bulged in his arms, chest, and shoulders. Scarlett wanted to reassure him that he was irresistibly attractive, even if his back was disfigured. It's what she would want to hear as a woman, but she doubted Griff cared if he was attractive to her, or to anyone else.

The silence lasted interminably, but she waited him out. She'd never sleep if she didn't know; she'd starred in too many action and thriller movies, and her imagination could go darker and more sadistic than what might have actually happened.

Finally, he grunted the words in a low, broken voice. "I was captured and imprisoned in Syria for a few weeks. They whipped us regularly, always on our backs, killed some of my men with the whip." He paused, and she wondered if he'd share more of what had happened, but he went on: "A couple years ago, I rescued Jasmine from a bomb and my back was burned in the explosion, adding to the scarring." He actually smiled then. "Didn't know that crazy woman would end up being my sister-in-law."

There were so many things she wanted to ask him right now—about the imprisonment, the torture, the men he'd lost, Jasmine—but from the way his face tightened, she was afraid she'd gotten all the info she could hope for.

Instead of asking more, she stepped in close, wrapped her arms around his lower back, and laid her head on his chest. Griff pulled in a quick breath, but he didn't pull away. He didn't return the hug, but it was enough that he let her stay close. The ridges and bumps underneath her palms and fingertips made her stomach queasy. *They whipped us regularly, killed some of my men.* She swallowed hard to keep the bile down. How many men had he lost in that imprisonment? Was that part of the reason he was so hard and unreachable?

Scarlett softly trailed her fingers over his lower back. Griff's body shuddered under her touch. She waited for him to run away from her. Long seconds passed where she ran her fingertips along the scars and savored the feel of his warm chest against her cheek. *Please hold me*, she thought, but she didn't voice it. This wasn't about her. It was about Griff knowing she wouldn't recoil from his scars, and she appreciated what he'd gone through for their country, and to save his sister-in-law. He was such a natural hero.

Griff muttered something she couldn't decipher, and then he wrapped his arms around her back and pulled her so close, she could hardly catch a full breath. Granted, part of her shortness of breath was due to his nearness and his reciprocation of her hug. He didn't move his hands, simply held her, but it was more than enough.

Time probably ticked by, but Scarlett didn't sense it. Her heart was cheering and her body knew it had found the spot it was meant to be in, close to the man she'd always loved.

Griff drew in a ragged breath and pulled back. Grasping her arms, he gently moved them from his back. "Good night, Jane," he whispered, but he didn't walk away. Still holding on to her forearms, he stared down at her as if he didn't want to leave.

Scarlett moistened her lips and waited.

Griff shook his head, released her arms, and hurried around her. Before she could blink, he was out her door and had closed it firmly behind him. She sank onto the bed, and tears welled up in her eyes: tears of selfishness for another rejection from Griff, and tears of sorrow for what he'd gone through and those men who'd been killed. She flung herself onto the pillow and cried until she blessedly fell asleep.

CHAPTER THIRTEEN

Griff suffered through another sleepless night. What was Scarlett doing to him? When she'd held him so tenderly and trailed her fingers over his scars, it had touched him deeply. His heart lightened just remembering it. His mama and sister, Navy, were great ladies, but they were a tough-love kind of people, and he'd shut himself off emotionally from even them years ago. He gave his mama, Navy, his nephew, and his sisters-in-law quick hugs when he saw them. Sometimes, when he had a break from work, he'd allow himself to go on a date and kiss a pretty girl. That was the extent of physical touch for him.

Ah, his Jane. Her outer beauty, which was world-acclaimed, had nothing on her inner beauty. After he'd reciprocated that hug last night, he'd known that he was still in love with her. Shouldn't years apart, most of his spent in hellish situations, harden him to the love of his younger life? He was certain it had, but Scarlett had once again penetrated his tough exterior.

He lay in bed later than usual, blinking at the sun streaming through the uncovered windows. They had automatic blinds for the windows in this house, but the only reason to ever shut them was if the sun glared too brightly off the snow. Griff didn't mind the glare, and he loved the sunshine. Scarlett was sunshine for him. She was so bright and beautiful that he should shield his eyes after all the darkness he'd been exposed to. Sadly for him, he'd rather go blind staring at her.

He heard her bedroom door open and close and then her shower start. She must've slipped out to go to the gym when he was dozing earlier from the long night of sleeplessness. That was his cue. He pushed out of bed, pulled on a T-shirt and some socks and shoes, and hurried for the gym.

As he pushed himself through his workout, last night played over and over again in his head. Scarlett had gotten him to talk about his scars and then had tenderly shown him that she accepted him. He was far from perfect, but Scarlett didn't care.

Yet his mind was also replaying everything that had happened with his brother, Kaleb, and his new wife, Jasmine. Griff had been the only one who related to Jasmine; she hadn't believed that she deserved a relationship with someone who was good and full of light. He related because that was part of the reason he'd ditched Scarlett years ago. There were so many reasons he couldn't be with her then, now, or ever.

He finished with weights and forced himself to do sprints on the treadmill, no matter how tired he was or how much he loathed running indoors. Sometimes if he sprinted hard and long enough, his lame brain would stop thinking.

He finished and downed a couple of water bottles before hurrying back to his suite. Luckily, he didn't see Scarlett. He was so close to breaking down with her, telling her secrets he'd never shared with anyone, holding her, admitting he loved her. He slammed into the bathroom and ripped off his shirt. Straining so he could see the puckered skin, he remembered the screams of his friends as they were beaten until they died. Only Griff and one other man had ultimately survived. He still hated his captors, would never forgive them for his friends' deaths, but sadly, he understood why they'd done it. Griff and his team had killed so many of their people—men, women, and even children who opposed them. Of course the Syrians needed retribution when they captured them.

Griff stared at himself in the mirror. His face was shadowed with a couple of days' growth. His beard came in darker than his hair. His eyes looked sunken and scared, and the sight made his temper flare up. Scarlett could not pierce his armor. She could not find out the secrets that no one knew aside from his team and their tormentors in Syria. She couldn't uncover the raw truth that everyone who'd ever served with him had discovered at some point.

He hurried into the shower, banging his head back against the marble enclosure. He wasn't right for Scarlett. If only he could make her understand that without hurting her any more. He'd hurt her plenty, breaking things off with her shortly after his first deployment with the Navy and never answering any of her emails or letters. The idea had been to protect her and allow her to have a life without the pain of loving and losing a warrior. He'd known he wasn't long for this world.

He'd loved Scarlett from afar for ten long years, and last night she'd told him that she'd always loved him too. He'd rather be whipped again than have to know he'd hurt her like that. Now he was doing it all over again: letting down his guard and holding her close, coming near to kissing her, only to pull away again. He hated himself for his weakness. The only thing he could do was sit her down and try to explain. The last thing he wanted to do was hurt her, but if she truly loved him, hurt was all that was in store for both of them.

Scarlett noticed Griff's door was closed when she went to work out and when she returned to her suite to shower. She put on a long-sleeved T-shirt and fitted yoga pants, not bothering with much makeup. Griff used to tell her he liked her face "clean and beautiful." She smiled in the mirror at the memory.

Had they had a breakthrough last night, or was he going to jilt her all over again this morning? She prayed for his heart to soften, but she was beginning to wonder if it was a vain repetition on her part. She'd prayed for Griff since they'd separated—for his protection, his happiness, and the long-held hope that he'd someday be returned to her. Only the good Lord knew where Griff's heart and head were. Who knew if he was capable of loving someone anymore? In a movie, it was so simple to change a character; with a big aha moment, a hardened warrior could change, soften, fall at the heroine's feet. Real life wasn't like that. She hated real life sometimes.

She went to the kitchen on the main level and made herself a yogurt parfait with frozen fruit and granola, leaving one for Griff in the fridge where he should see it. Then she padded downstairs to the huge theater room. She'd spent a lot of time near the fireplace in the office on the main level reading through the Shaffers' David Baldacci and Clive Cussler novels, but she couldn't focus on a book when her brain was scrambled by Griff. Maybe a movie could distract her, or it could put her to sleep. Goodness knew she hadn't slept much in the past four days.

As she searched through the movies, she saw the shelf full of Wii games. She'd noticed the sensor bar on top of the huge television. Hmm. *Just Dance* would be a lot of fun. Within minutes, she was dancing along with the game. It was exactly the tonic she needed to make her smile and make her forget about her pain for a few minutes. It would be even more fun with a friend, but Griff kept making it clear he wasn't her friend.

Griff walked into the great room area, looking around for Scarlett. He wanted to see her, but it would be much smarter if he stayed away. He made it to the kitchen and found the yogurt parfait she'd made for him. She was so thoughtful. Over the past few days, he'd watched through the security cameras as she worked diligently in the kitchen, and after she'd vacate the kitchen, he'd find the delicious food she left for him. She'd always been a good cook, and he appreciated the kindness. If only he could thank her without grabbing her and kissing her.

He scrambled some eggs to go with the parfait, but he paused when music floated up from the basement. He wondered what

Scarlett was doing, and he had to force himself to down the eggs, the parfait, and some milk, then run upstairs to brush his teeth, before going to investigate.

He called himself a lot of names as he pumped down the stairs to the basement. He wanted to be with Scarlett, despite all the reasons he shouldn't be—and the biggest reason was that he didn't want to hurt her again.

Hurrying through the short hall, he could hear the music getting louder. "Girls Just Wanna Have Fun." He smiled. His older sister, Navy, had loved this old eighties song.

He reached the door to the theater, where his steps faltered. Scarlett's back was to him. She faced the large screen, following the dance moves. If he'd thought her stretching outside of the bathroom in Nephi and saying "bum" was hard to resist, this was torture. She danced, she shimmied, she moved in ways no beautiful woman should move, if she wanted the man in her life to stay sane. His Jane was sexy and adorable at the same time. Griff loved her so much.

Griff had been frozen for almost half a minute before he realized he had to act—either retreat up the stairs and lock himself in his room, or get her to stop dancing. He made a poor choice as he rushed into the theater, wrapped his arms around her from behind, and said gruffly in her ear, "Stop."

Scarlett let out a little squeal of surprise, but then she did the worst possible thing: she started dancing again within the circle of his arms.

Griff tightened his grip on her. Her upper body stilled, but her lower body kept swaying to the beat. "You've got to stop," he begged.

Scarlett tilted her head back and locked gazes with him over her shoulder. "Why?" she asked, all innocence and beauty.

"I can't take much more," he admitted, then immediately regretted it when she grinned.

That grin made his arms weaken enough for her to spin in his embrace, continue swaying her hips, and say, "Dance with me, Griff."

Griff stayed firmly planted in one spot, but he was spineless enough he kept his arms around her, savored each movement of her body against his. This was wrong, and he knew it. His mama would cuss him for his impure thoughts. His sister would cuss him for not dancing with Scarlett and taking it to the next level.

"No!" Griff roared. He released her from his arms and took a large step back.

Scarlett startled, looking stunned, and she finally, finally stopped dancing. Her green eyes shone, and Griff felt horror rush through him as he realized she was going to cry. He was a man, so of course he hated seeing any woman cry, but seeing Scarlett cry was torture. The Syrians would be laughing in the mass grave he'd placed them in.

"You can't even stand to be close to me, can you?" she said in a quiet voice he barely heard over the music.

Griff didn't know how to protest. Being close to her was heaven, but he was destined for an eternity in the other direction. He couldn't bring her with him on that trip.

Scarlett waited, as if hoping he'd contradict her. A single tear crested her thick eyelashes and trickled down her cheek. What Griff wouldn't give to kiss that tear away, to hold her and take away her pain ...

She let out a soft sob and ran around him. Griff leaned his head back, clenched his fists, and groaned. Why did he keep hurting her like this? He hated himself, and he had to somehow stop this pattern.

He picked up the remote and shut off the television. Then he dropped his head to his chest, staying there and wallowing in the pain for a while before muttering a quick prayer. He knew the Lord didn't want to hear from him, but of course He cared about someone as good as Scarlett. "Please help me explain," he murmured. He wanted to beg for help not to hurt her anymore, but he knew this was going to hurt her. There was no way around it now. He had to plunge this dagger into Scarlett and pray she could move on and find happiness, knowing he cared for her too much to be with her.

Griff slowly walked out of the theater. The burden of truth weighed heavily on him. He wished he could simply love Scarlett and ease her pain that way. He'd have to be content with the truth. Sadly, he knew she wouldn't. He knew she wanted him, and he could never give himself to anyone, even Scarlett.

CHAPTER FOURTEEN

Scarlett should've run for her room, but she couldn't stand being closed in there right now. She was humiliated that she'd let Griff see her cry. The ache for Griff just kept growing and growing until her chest felt tight and she couldn't seem to clear her lungs. She stormed to the mudroom off the garage and shrugged into Tucker's coat and boots, all of which swallowed her up. Luckily, some of Maryn's gloves fit on her hands. Scarlett wasn't a big person, but Maryn Shaffer was miniscule.

She pushed out the exterior door of the mudroom. The air nipped at her face, but as she slammed the door and trudged onto the spacious rear patio, she felt like she could breathe again. She'd been cooped up inside for far too long.

It was picturesque out here. Trees towered above her, their branches laden with white fluff. The river danced over icy rocks. Even though it was cold, she could see spring was coming and hear water dripping out of the rain gutters as the snow started to melt in the bright sunshine.

Scarlett saw a trail broken through the snow that approached the river. She went down the steps from the patio and slowly followed it; walking in these massive boots was awkward. At least the coat kept her warm. She reached the river and paused for a second, listening to the water and relishing the sun on her face. She was calming down, but her stomach still churned from Griff's roar of *No!* He truly must despise her to treat her the way he had. She brushed at her cheeks with the back of the long coat sleeve and trudged along the bank of the river, moving away from the house. The snow wasn't as thick if she stayed close to the water.

Suddenly, a deer bounded into view on the opposite bank. Scarlett halted and watched the beautiful white-tailed creature. She loved deer; they seemed so blissfully unaware. It was pathetic that she wished she could have an existence like that. She smiled at her silly thoughts as the deer broke ground to the river and then drank from it.

It paused in its drinking, and its head darted up. The large brown eyes stared right at Scarlett. She wanted to tell it not to bound off, that she wouldn't hurt it, but movement pulled her gaze from the deer.

Scarlett's own eyes widened as she saw a pack of wolves pushing through the snow from each direction. They were going to trap the deer and slaughter it right before her eyes. It looked like something out of a Western movie she'd acted in where wolves silently surrounded her as she'd played a tough frontierswoman. She'd read up on wolves' behavior and responses and how to best them for her part. Her character had fought her way free with fire and a stick. Scarlett had no stick or fire right now, and she knew these wolves wouldn't be cowed by her small stature. Yet she had to do something to help the deer.

"Run!" she screamed at the helpless animal, breaking the silence of the winter landscape.

The deer startled and bounded across the river toward her. Scarlett cried out in horror as she realized two things: the river wasn't as deep as she'd thought and wouldn't slow the wolves down at all, and that deer was much faster than her. She didn't want the deer to be hurt, but she definitely didn't want a pack of wolves chasing her.

In sync, the wolves focused in on her, snarled, and pushed through the deep snow toward the river. The deer darted past her into the trees. Some supporting character that animal turned out to be.

Scarlett had no choice. She slipped out of the heavy boots and sprinted in her socks back along the riverbank. The icy path with rocks jutting out at odd intervals stung at her feet, but she pushed on. The wolves reached the river, started cutting across it, and spread out to flank her on both sides. In seconds, they would close in on her. She sadly couldn't remember any of the research she'd done on wolves for her part in that stupid, unrealistic movie.

She clung to the hope that she could reach the trail by the cabin before the wolves overtook her. If only Griff would appear and save her. Thinking of that gave her the only good idea she'd had today. She drew in a breath and screamed, "Help!"

Griff left the theater and started searching the house for Scarlett. It was a big shift from the past three days where he'd avoided her if at all possible. She wasn't in the kitchen, the living area, the office, or her room. Her bedroom door was open, and he made the mistake of walking all the way in, just to make sure she wasn't there. He could smell her clean, fresh scent. Not the expensive perfume she'd worn the first time he'd seen her again, but that peaches-and-cream scent she used to emanate when they were dating in college. He smirked to himself. Apparently she'd used the shampoo, conditioner, body wash, and lotion he'd bought at Wal-Mart.

He looked outside the large windows. Scarlett wouldn't have gone out in the cold, would she? She didn't have the right gear, and although there was still a thick layer of snow, it was spring and the animals were coming out, most of them desperately hungry from either hibernation or a long winter.

He hurried to the windows and searched. At first he only saw a world of white and trees and the river cutting through it all, but then a body moved into his view from the right. It was Scarlett, and she was sprinting. At the same moment, he saw the pack of wolves cutting through the river toward her. At deeper spots a few of them got thrown off the path and had to swim for a second, but they found their footing and kept coming. By the way they fanned out, he could tell they were on the hunt.

Griff's stomach tightened and ice ran down his spine. Scarlett! He sprinted through the house, pounding down the stairs. Tucker kept his guns locked in the safe in the basement. Griff had stupidly left his gun in his bedroom, and there was no way he was wasting precious seconds and going back for it. Griff yanked a couple of knives from a block in the kitchen as he rushed through, then kept running out the rear patio doors.

Scarlett appeared on the trail that cut back to the house, but the wolves were exiting the river now and almost upon her. Running away from them was the worst thing she could do. Wolves thought anything that ran was prey. Griff flew across the path to the river, praying inside like he hadn't prayed since Syria. God hadn't listened then, and Griff was terrified He wouldn't listen now.

CHAPTER FIFTEEN

Scarlett could almost feel the wolves snapping at her heels as she reached the path that led back to the house. Stupidly, she looked over her shoulder. They'd exited the river and were padding silently toward her, intent on their target. Maybe twenty feet separated them from her, and they were coming fast.

She tripped and screamed out as she rolled and slammed into the snow at the side of the trail. Horror rushed through her as she curled into a ball and prayed. They were going to rip her apart. Now she remembered one stupid fact—wolves went for the neck and the jugular. Her character in the movie had fought them. Scarlett had no weapons or hope at all.

"Hey!" a loud voice hollered above her. Scarlett looked up to see Griff's determined face as he leapt over her and planted himself between her and the wolves. "Go!" he yelled even louder, rotating to face each of them straight on.

She stared up at him. He looked terrifying and awe-inspiring in a short-sleeved T-shirt and brandishing two kitchen knives. Would that be enough to help him win against a pack of wolves? The research she'd done for her movie was coming back to her now, and she remembered there had been no real-life cases of a human beating a pack without fire and some serious weapons. Yet if anyone could take on wolves with only kitchen knives and sheer strength, it would be Griff.

She focused on the wolves. They'd stopped about ten feet away. They were snarling now and eyeing Griff, as if trying to decide whether eating Scarlett was worth this fight.

Griff waved the knives, puffed himself up, standing on tiptoes in his socks in the snow, and let out a roar powerful enough to shake snow off of nearby trees. A couple of the wolves howled back. Was he going to scare them away or make them want to fight him? He was an alpha through and through. Didn't wolves want to challenge the alpha? She wanted to cling to him and drag him back to the safety of the cabin.

"Stand up and slowly back away," Griff said quietly to her.

Scarlett obeyed, standing and taking a couple of steps back. "Come with me," she begged.

Griff seemed to listen as he eased back with her, still standing large and intimidating as ever, at least to a human. She knew wolves only thought in terms of prey and who they could best. As a pack, they might believe they could take Griff down, no matter how large and tough he appeared.

The wolves started carefully, cautiously spreading wider, working their way through the snow. Scarlett's stomach plunged. There were six of them. They could easily circle behind Scarlett and Griff, cutting off their escape. She hated real life so much right now. Living vicariously through something like this in a movie was definitely the way to go.

"Back up faster," Griff instructed, "but don't run or turn around."

Scarlett realized the mistake she'd made. Running meant she was prey. She'd learned that when she was researching for her frontierswoman role, but learning facts and implementing them in real life were two very different things. She'd like to see whoever wrote that research face off against a pack of terrifying wolves.

Scarlett kept easing back, and Griff kept yelling, growling, and waving the knives around. The wolves steadily tracked them, close to completing the circle all the way around them. It was a slower progression for the ones not on the trail, but they kept up as Scarlett didn't dare move too fast.

She risked a glance over her shoulder and saw the patio was only about ten feet away. They might make it.

The lead wolf let out a howl, and the rest of the pack answered it. The hairs on the back of Scarlett's neck stood on end. What did that howl mean? She didn't have to wait long to know; the wolves flew at them.

"Run!" Griff yelled. Scarlett didn't need to be told twice. She darted across the path, up the patio steps and onto the wide patio, dodging around the furniture that was covered for the winter.

Griff was right behind her. The lead wolf leapt at Griff. Griff dodged to the side, and the wolf slammed into an outdoor couch.

"Go!" Griff hollered at her, turning to face the wolf, but the animal was closest to her, the rest of the pack not far behind in their attack.

Scarlett couldn't leave Griff, but what help could she be with snarling wolves ready to rip her throat out? The throat. That was it. She remembered more real-life trivia that might actually be helpful. Dodging at the main wolf, which she assumed was the alpha, she heard Griff cry out for her from behind as she plunged her fist into the wolf's mouth and down his throat. His teeth scratched through the coat and tore at the flesh of her arm, but she kept pushing, thankful she had gloves on so she couldn't feel how disgusting his throat probably was.

The wolf struggled to get free, whipping its head back and forth, but she worked out hard every day and the winter must've been vicious for these wolves. He wasn't as strong as she was, not to mention the fact that he couldn't breathe as she kept pushing her fist down his throat until she was up to her elbow. She turned her head away so she didn't have to look at the beast, gritting her teeth and pushing hard with her legs to stay in place.

Griff was right next to her, moving as if to pull her away from the wolf, but the other wolves were upon them now.

"I've got him!" she screamed, pushing and pushing, though inside she wanted to curl in a ball and cry. It was horrific to have her arm down this wolf's throat, but he couldn't snap his jaw shut with the way she was pushing and it was obvious he couldn't breathe.

Griff turned and shoved both his knives into the closest wolf. The wolf howled in pain, and Griff kicked it away. It scuttled back from the fight, the knives protruding from its mangy coat. Scarlett had to concentrate on keeping her fist planted in this wolf's throat. A large covered couch was nearby. She rotated slowly to brace her legs against it and jammed her fist as deep as she could.

More wolves were coming fast. Griff lifted a patio chair and hurled it at them. The chair took out three of them, and they yelped and scurried back from the battle. The fourth one paused, as if surveying the fight. Now that it didn't have the strength of the pack to back it up, would it keep fighting?

Griff faced it and hollered so loud it hurt Scarlett's ears. "Go!" Then he stood so strong and brave, his arms high above his head, every muscle in his neck, shoulders, and arms popping.

Scarlett knew she'd never seen a hero as impressive as Griff.

"Go!" he yelled again.

The wolf slowly backed away.

Griff sidled closer to her, keeping his arms up and his posture threatening. "Pull your arm back and run for the house," he said in a calm voice.

She knew not to argue with him, but what if the wolf got Griff, or the others rebounded once their leader was free?

"Now!" he commanded.

Scarlett pulled her arm free, and the wolf snapped at her. Griff kicked it hard in the ribs and sent it sprawling off the patio. Scarlett ran for the door, flinging it open. Griff was right behind her, pushing her through. He slammed it shut behind him and twisted the dead bolt.

They both whirled to watch the wolves. The pack stood there uncertainly for a few seconds; then they scurried back down the trail to the river. The one with the knives sticking out of its back brought up the rear, limping. Would that one die? Scarlett certainly wasn't going after it to pull the knives out.

She released a pent-up breath and muttered, "I'm never going outside again."

Griff turned to her, shaking his head and staring at her in wonder. "You were brilliant! You were absolutely amazing!"

Scarlett's jaw dropped. Back in college, Griff had often told her how impressive she was, but to see him this animated blew her away.

Griff put both hands under her arms and lifted her into the air like she was the champion. Scarlett felt weak with relief that the battle was over, but she was even weaker with surprise at how Griff was reacting.

He gazed up at her, grinning. "You're tougher than any action hero."

Scarlett's nerves were gradually settling, but she couldn't think what to say.

Griff lowered her to her feet, kissed her so quickly she barely realized it was happening before it was over, and then gave her a fierce hug. "Oh, Jane," he murmured against her hair. "You're really all right. I was so scared."

The words coming out of his mouth were so foreign for Griff, Scarlett couldn't even return the hug or fully process that the love of her life was finally, finally holding her tightly against him. Had he really kissed her? Her lips were saying yes, but it had been too fast and she wondered if she was in shock from the fight with the wolves and Griff's reaction.

Griff pulled back slightly, smiling down at her. "You are amazing, Scarlett Lily. Show that true-life scene to your fans, and they'd be prostrate on the ground worshipping you. I guess they already do, right?"

Scarlett shook her head and whispered, "Griff. What happened to you?"

His grin faltered, but he still held her close and stared at her like she was his idol or something. "I'm gushing, aren't I? I sound like Kaleb or Ryder right now, but if you could've seen yourself jamming your fist down the alpha male's throat ... How did you think of that?"

"I read up on wolves when I was preparing for a part, and that tidbit just came to me." She needed to say lots of prayers of gratitude right now. The Lord had obviously protected them.

"Brilliant." He smiled again. "Now I sound like Sutton. Next I'll be saying 'cheers.'"

She could see he was gradually calming down and returning to the gruff Griff that she knew and, despite herself, loved.

"Not too brilliant," she admitted. "I should've known not to run."

He lifted his shoulders. "You couldn't have taken on a pack by yourself."

"You could have. You were amazing out there."

"Thanks." Griff's shutter fell over his eyes. His arms dropped to his side, and he stepped back. Scarlett felt the loss of his touch all through her body. "That terrified me," he admitted.

Scarlett nodded in agreement. She felt weak and exhausted and her arm stung. Glancing down, she saw where the wolf's teeth had scraped through the heavy coat; blood was seeping out in a few places.

Griff followed her gaze and cursed. He escorted her to the kitchen sink, gently slid the heavy coat off of her, and let it drop to the floor.

Scarlett looked down at her arm. It wasn't too bad, considering. Drops of blood beaded through her torn sleeve.

Griff took off her gloves and slid the shirt carefully up to her elbow. When she winced, his gaze flew to her face. "I'm sorry."

"I'm tough," she insisted.

Griff smiled briefly. "Yes, you are, but your fans are going to cry if this perfect arm has scars."

"Gives character." She couldn't take her eyes from Griff's face as he returned her gaze. His scars were a part of him and she hated that he'd been hurt, but she wanted to love all of him. How could she convey that without him shutting himself away again?

Finally, he nodded and turned from her. Pulling a clean cloth out, he ran it under the water, squeezed it, and then tenderly pressed it to the thin cuts. She doubted they would need stitches, and there were only four scrapes. She might need rabies shots when they returned to civilization, but she would be fine.

He studied the cloth on her arm as she studied him. He was the most handsome man she'd ever seen, but the depth of Griff pulled her in more surely than his perfect face. Reaching up with her other hand, she cupped his face. His eyes darted up again.

"Thank you for coming for me," she said.

Griff's blue gaze warmed her clear through. Any other hero would say they'd always come for her, or something similar. Not Griff. That was okay. He'd come. She didn't need flowery words. She needed him.

The moment was beautiful, and Griff seemed invested in her. This was it; she could feel it. He'd lean down, capture her lips with his, and her world would upend. He did lean down. Her breath caught in her throat, and her heart thumped louder than when she'd been running from a pack of wolves.

Griff suddenly lifted the washcloth from her arm, bent down low, and kissed right next to one of the cuts. His lips on her arm did crazy things to her insides. If only he'd work his way up to her face. He glanced up at her, his eyes smoldering with love and desire ... for her. She knew it! Four days alone and Griff had returned to her. She had no desire to gloat, only to hold him and talk through all the years and pain, and find the joy of being together again.

Slowly, Griff straightened, and she couldn't resist tracing her eyes over the impressive muscles in his chest and shoulders. She met his gaze, and he lowered his head close to hers. His warm breath brushed her cheek. Scarlett arched up toward him, but she would not cross those final centimeters. It had to be him. He had to rescue her from the loneliness and anguish that he'd created by deserting her.

Griff softly, achingly brushed his lips over hers. Scarlett trembled at his tenderness. Griff wasn't tender; he was a warrior at heart. She knew he could be tender with her, and she loved that that hadn't changed. She waited for more, but Griff didn't move. Her eyes fluttered open to see that his gaze was intent on her.

His face softened, and he cupped her cheek with his hand, tenderly brushing his thumb along her jaw. "Jane," he murmured.

She gave him an encouraging smile. She was waiting, ready, and able to kiss away all their heartache, pain, and loss. She loved him. It didn't matter what they'd been through, or how much junk they needed to work through. Now if only he'd finally kiss her and start their path to healing.

"We need to talk," he murmured.

"I know." She had so much to say to him, so much of her future to plan with him.

He straightened, distancing his face from her lips. Out of her reach, once again.

"What are you doing?" she cried out.

He blinked down at her. "We both agreed we need to talk."

"Not right now," she protested. "Honestly, Griff! You suck as a leading man, you know that?"

Griff smiled, which infuriated her even more.

She pulled her hand from his face and jabbed it in his chest. "Don't you smile at me. You know how long I've been waiting for your kiss, how patient I've been? And then you barely brush my lips and move away. How can you be so heroic in every way but the one that really matters?"

Griff's smile fled. He grunted, shook his head, and walked away from her.

"Where are you going?" she demanded.

"To get some Steri-Strips for your arm," he threw over his shoulder, not stopping.

She focused on calming breaths, but she'd need hours of yoga with a master to take away this anguish. No, nothing but Griff could take it away, and he didn't seem inclined to love her anytime soon.

Griff went to the mudroom and returned with a first-aid kit. He irrigated the cuts, dried them, put on antibiotic cream, and carefully Steri-Stripped them closed, all the while focused on her arm and not even looking at her face. Which was probably just as well—she was sure her face was red with anger and humiliation.

He finished and cleaned up the supplies, put the first aid kit away, deposited Tucker's coat and Maryn's gloves in the laundry room, and then retrieved two water bottles from the fridge. She simply watched him the entire time, resentment and despair battling within her. Most of her life was spent in a fantasy world. She recognized this, but was it really that hard for her real-life hero to apologize for deserting her and then give her a decent kiss? Good criminy, he was infuriating.

Griff walked to her and handed her one of the water bottles.

"Thanks," she muttered, twisting off the cap and taking a long drink.

"Can we go down to the theater to talk?" he asked, draining half of his water bottle and then setting it on the counter.

"Why the theater?" At least he wasn't dodging their talk now. She wasn't going to get the kisses and love she'd dreamed of, but maybe she'd get some answers.

Griff looked her over and admitted quietly, "You're like sunshine to me." He gestured to the sun pouring through the huge windows. "I can only handle so much light."

Okay, that was pretty sweet, and illuminating. She had awful visions of him stuck in a dirty, dark prison, his tormentors only pulling him out to whip him. If she was sunshine to him, and he couldn't handle light ... She gasped. "That's why you don't want me anymore?"

Griff chuckled, deep and low, and he brushed the hair from her neck. Her skin tingled in response, and her heart leapt at the simple touch. "Don't overthink it, Jane. I want you plenty."

Scarlett about flung her arms around his neck, not caring that her one arm was injured. The bites were superficial anyway. As if sensing her intentions, he cut off her hope of going for a better kiss this time by wrapping his arm around her waist and escorting her toward the front entry and the stairs. Neither of them said anything as they walked down the stairs together, passed through the short hall, and finally settled into a leather couch side by side in the darkened theater.

She wanted to ask him question after question, but she waited.

Finally, Griff muttered, "I guess this is my party, right?"

Scarlett smiled. "You did issue the invite."

Griff took one of her hands between both of his, which both thrilled her and gave her hope. Maybe this was the breakthrough she'd been praying for. She'd get hunted by wolves every day if it brought Griff to her side. Well, maybe not every day, but at least once a week.

She smiled tremulously at him. "I love your hands," she said.

Griff rubbed his thumb along the back of her hand. "I used to love to hold yours."

Scarlett's chest warmed. He hadn't cast what they'd had from his memory. She wanted to pile him with questions, but she held back, worried what the answers might be. Loving Griff Quinn was a tremendous amount of work, but she'd never shied away from hard work. Especially when she knew the results would be well worth the effort. Patience and restraint were of the essence right now. If they failed her, she was going to plant herself on his lap and kiss him until he couldn't deny their love any longer, or pushed her onto the floor.

Griff swallowed and, clinging to her hand, said, "I realized late last night how much I've hurt you, am still hurting you."

Scarlett pulled back slightly. "This was a startling revelation to you?"

"Yeah. I'd hoped you'd forgotten about me with your busy, glamorous life and moved on."

How could he be so impressive and so stupid and insulting all at the same time? "Griff, I love you, but you are a stupid jerk sometimes."

Griff pulled in a slow breath and pushed it out. He released her hands and said quietly, "Please, Scarlett. Don't tell me you love me. This is hard enough."

She gasped and slapped him hard across the jaw. Griff didn't flinch, and he didn't even have the graciousness to look insulted or upset.

Scarlett leapt to her feet and clenched her fists. "'This is hard enough'? You don't even know what hard is, you jerk! Do you have any clue what I've suffered through the past ten years? Loving you, missing you, being deserted by you?"

Griff stood slowly to face her. A muscle worked in his jaw, and he splayed his hands as if to placate her. "That's why I'm trying to talk to you now. Explain why we can't be together so I don't hurt you anymore."

"Ha." She pushed out a huffy breath and glared at him. "You claim you don't want to hurt me? Well, you are! Every minute of every day, you hurt me. The only way you *won't* hurt me is by finally loving me."

She threw the words out there like bullets, but somehow they didn't hit their target. They floated around in the air between them and then settled to the carpet, harmless, ineffective, lame. He obviously didn't love her. She should appreciate that he didn't want to hurt her, but what did that help when he was ripping her apart by not returning her love?

"I'm sorry," he muttered.

"Argh!" She screamed, threw her hands in the air, and stomped around him. She got to the theater door and turned back. "You should've let the wolves rip my jugular out. It would've been less painful for both of us!"

"Jane," he murmured, his blue eyes dark with pain.

"My name is Scarlett!" With that final scream, she ran from the room, down the hallway, up the two flights of stairs, and into her bedroom.

She slammed the door and locked it, but that didn't seem like enough. Dragging the closest dresser in front of the door took a few minutes, but she was strong enough to punch her fist down a wolf's throat; she could move this stupid dresser. She grunted and pushed, and it slowly moved into place. Even Griff couldn't get through that door. She grunted with satisfaction and brushed her hands.

She stood there looking at the dresser, at the door, waiting, waiting. He should come, try to bang down the door. Nothing. Not a footstep on the stairs. Her chest heaved with emotion and exertion. Why? How could he be incapable of feeling anything for her? Scarlett wearily sank to her knees, uttering a desperate prayer to understand where Griff was coming from. Especially since she'd thrown a fit and hadn't let him explain. It just hurt so much that she couldn't even tell him she loved him and she'd finally snapped, slapping him, yelling at him, and then running away. She wasn't proud of her reaction, and she needed help forgiving and relating to him.

She closed her eyes tightly, and her heart twisted as she envisioned Griff in his darkest hours: body splayed wide, his hands and feet tied to posts, and his bare back being shredded by a whip, blood dripping down to the ground. He didn't cry out; he didn't react at all. His jaw was clenched and his body taut. The only emotion was in his eyes—raw fury and retribution. When he got loose, he was going to kill his tormentors.

Griff's men were bound at either side of him, sagging against their bonds. They were either dead or dying. And there was nothing he could do but watch as the whip cracked again.

Scarlett crumpled to the floor and sobbed as she felt a mere taste of what Griff had felt. He was desperate, alone, and filled with torment. His anger wasn't for his pain or his torture. It was for his men.

She curled into a ball and continued to weep for him. No wonder he couldn't love her. Maybe it hadn't happened like she was imagining, but whatever had happened had scarred him more deeply than what she'd seen on his back. Too deeply to recover. The man she loved was gone, and she was living in a fantasy world if she thought he'd ever return.

CHAPTER SIXTEEN

Griff berated himself for his careless treatment of Scarlett, once again. Maybe he just couldn't communicate all of his issues in a way that wouldn't further break her heart. He couldn't believe he'd been so naïve to take this job and assume he could remain detached. Some part of his hardened heart had recognized, even before he agreed to protect her, how deep Scarlett was inside of him. His Jane. The only love he'd ever had.

He was a careless, selfish idiot. Sutton had dozens of men who could've done this op, protected Scarlett, and not emotionally wounded her over and over again. He wanted to run upstairs, bang open her door, and just hold her, but that would only make her hurt worse when he had to walk away, and especially when he was killed. Walk away he would. A man like him had no business loving anyone, let alone an angel like Scarlett. She deserved so much.

Kneeling down in the darkened theater, he found himself returning to his roots, praying like his parents and pastor had taught him. He started with thanking the Lord for protecting Scarlett from the wolves. That battle had divine intervention written all over it, and Griff couldn't deny it any more than he could deny how much he loved the tough woman who had punched her fist down the alpha wolf's throat. That memory would never leave him, just like dozens more of his Jane. She was unreal.

After he muttered out his gratitude as eloquently as he could, he begged the Lord to help Scarlett to forgive him, to heal her pain, to help her to move on and forget Griff, and—last and most painful of all—to find a man worthy of her beautiful, giving heart and untarnished soul.

He finished and hoped for some warm approval or something like he'd been taught he should feel. Nothing came. He glared up at the ceiling. "What do you want from me? I know I'm a monster, but I've worked and sacrificed to protect those who can't protect themselves, to try to atone for brutally taking lives. I've tried." He rested his head on his forearms, and hate boiled in him again. Not for his captors. Not for a hundred other ops in the military and working for Sutton where he'd dealt with evil, depraved people. It was always kill or be killed for him, and he instinctively put himself in the worst situations possible.

This intense loathing was only directed at himself. He hated what he'd become. He hated that because of the atrocities he'd committed and the way he reacted in battle, he could never find happiness, never be with his Jane again. Most of all, he hated himself for the hurt he saw in her beautiful green eyes.

Scarlett went through the rest of the day in a painful haze. She didn't leave her room, didn't eat, didn't run through the house searching for Griff like she wanted to. She'd been given that insight into what he'd gone through, and it felt very, very real to her. Her stomach was sick, her forehead was burning, and her back ached like it had been shredded by that whip. She prayed she was coming down with the flu. How wonderful would that be to just crawl into bed and be out of her head for a few days? Maybe the person who instigated her hit would be caught and she could escape this beautiful place with vicious wolves outside and the man she loved inside. The man who was incapable of loving her back. She didn't blame him anymore for being so hardened to her and to her love, but it still was a miserable reality she lived in right now.

Darkness mercifully crept across the landscape below her window. As she'd stared out her window today at the river and trail below, she could see bright red spots where the wounded wolf had left his mark, and she remembered watching Griff fighting for her. He was such a superhero. That had to be part of why they couldn't be together. She might pretend to be heroic, but Griff was a true hero. He'd given his life to protect others, and a life like that wasn't conducive to love and soft touches.

She groaned, more agony rolling through her as she lost him all over again. It seemed even worse to her than when he'd ditched her years ago, but maybe that was just because it was the present and the old wounds had started to heal.

She moved the stupid dresser back away from the door and then started a bath, thinking maybe it would feel good. Searching through the cupboards, she found lavender bath salts and poured them in. If anything could help her sleep, she'd be so grateful. She'd been stupid not to put sleeping pills of some sort on that list for Griff to buy. She should've realized being cooped up with him would make it impossible to sleep peacefully.

As the large jetted tub filled, she stared dully around the spacious bathroom. Her gaze settled on the bottle of blonde hair dye on the counter. She smiled for what felt like the first time in days. A trip down memory lane was silly, but she wanted to say goodbye to Griff in a way that he would always remember. A trip down memory lane might at least get him to open up to her so she could show him that she would always love him, even if he couldn't return it.

Picking up the bottle, she opened it, pulled everything out, and started reading the directions.

CHAPTER SEVENTEEN

Griff slept, which was another gift from above. He still felt groggy as he awakened, though, and he wanted nothing more than to run dozens of miles in the crisp air outside, but he couldn't leave Scarlett. He put on a shirt, shorts, socks, and shoes and slipped out of his room. Weights and the treadmill would have to substitute for an outside run today.

Scarlett's door was still closed. She'd spent the rest of the afternoon and evening in her room yesterday. Would she emerge today? He wanted to better explain himself, but he was afraid he'd muddle it all up and injure her tender heart even worse.

As he descended the stairs to the basement, he heard the cable machine weights clack together in the gym. Scarlett was in there. He should turn around and give her space, but his stubborn feet kept carrying him toward the gym. When he cleared the doorframe, his feet finally stopped and rooted to the floor. His jaw dropped open as well.

Scarlett flipped her long, now honey-blonde hair over her shoulder and turned his way with a brilliant smile. "Good morning, Griff." She was bright, fresh, and beautiful. She had no makeup on, and her clear green eyes sparkled at him. How he loved her blonde, her natural color. How he loved her without makeup and in a simple T-shirt and shorts. How he loved her.

"Oh, Jane," he sort of groaned out.

She smiled brightly. "Do you like it?"

"Do I *like* it?" He rushed across the space between them. He reached her, and she tilted her head up and grinned at him. Griff ran his fingers through her hair. It was as silky and enchanting as he remembered. "You're so beautiful," he murmured.

Scarlett's bright smile changed to a knowing look that pulled him in even further. She knew what she was doing to him, but he sensed it wasn't to trick him into anything. Perhaps it was a gift, helping him remember their love and innocence. He'd loved her and known he was going to go out and save the world. The plans had been twisted and scorched in the horrors of reality, but Jane's love still shone through it all.

"Jane," he moaned, his hands entangled in her hair. He gently pulled her closer to him. "I want to kiss you and love you. I wish I could explain how much I want to, but if I do, I'll just hurt you worse when I leave again."

She nodded and gave him a tremulous smile. "I know, Griff."

He cocked his head to the side. "What do you mean, you know?"

She swallowed. "I had ... a vision, I guess you could call it." Her voice lowered. "I saw you being whipped. I saw the men next to you dead. I felt your anger at your captors. I understand why you've been so hardened that you don't think you can return to me."

Griff released his grip on her and backed away.

Her eyes widened, but she didn't falter. "It doesn't matter, Griff. I know your honor, your goodness, your—"

"I'm not good," he cut her off.

"Yes, you are." She stepped up to him. "And I'll love you, no matter what. I know you'll have to leave me again. I know you have to save the world. All I care is that, if you can, you come back again."

Griff's heart hammered painfully against his chest. Her love was the most precious gift, but he couldn't take it. All that would do was give her more pain in the end. Was the Lord even listening to his prayers? Jane needed to forget him and move on, not pledge her love, pledge to wait for him as he did suicidal undercover assignments, took down trafficking rings, drug lords, and mafia families. He'd tried since Syria not to kill if he didn't have to, but sometimes it was necessary, and someday soon he'd be killed in an op. He'd known that simple fact since his early days in the military when everyone around him, including himself, had discovered it was his natural reaction to run into danger, to go in when others were headed the other way. Yet if Scarlett had truly seen what happened in Syria, she'd understand part of the reasons why he had to stay away. How dark he'd become.

"You saw me in Syria?" he asked, his voice raw and painful.

She nodded.

"Did you see what happened before our imprisonment?"

She shook her head slightly.

If she hadn't seen that, she hadn't seen the deepest part of the darkness inside him. If he ever wanted her to give up on him, he had to show her. "You didn't see all the people my men and I were ordered to kill?" It hurt so much to talk about this. "Men, women, children."

Her lovely face blanched and she leaned against the cable machine. "Who ordered you to kill them?"

"Our superior officers."

"You can't be held accountable for that," she said quietly.

"I did it!" he roared back at her, and she shrank away from him. Griff pushed at his short hair. "I'm sorry, Scarlett. I'm sorry."

She stared at him, as if unsure who he was or what she was seeing.

"You saw us being whipped? You saw my men dead?" he asked her again. He wanted to stop now, but he couldn't. The Lord had given her a partial vision of what he'd been through, but she needed the complete picture. A voice in his head whispered, "*Stop*," but Griff was far past listening.

She nodded, her eyes wide.

"Did you see me pretend to faint?"

Her eyes registered confusion.

"Did you see them loosen my bonds?"

She shook her head slightly.

Griff walked slowly toward her. The memories were all rushing back, and he needed her to understand the monster he was. He couldn't simply love her, marry her, tell her, *See you in a few months, honey, while I go dismantle the refuse of the earth*, then come back all cheery and in love. It was not possible, no matter how deeply he loved her. He stopped a foot away from her.

"If you'd seen the end of the story," he said in a low, gravelly voice, "you would've seen me slaughter them. All of them. When they were all dead, I freed my men and buried most of them. Only two of my men were still alive: Jimmy and Trace. By the time I found a copter and flew us to safety, Jimmy was gone. Trace has never been the same. He's in a mental institution. His PTSD is so bad he can't function."

Scarlett's green eyes brimmed with sympathy.

Griff closed his own eyes so he wouldn't have to see her pity. "Don't feel bad for me, please." He opened his eyes because she needed to see his sincerity when he said the next part. "I tried to explain last night—poorly, I admit—how I don't want to hurt you anymore."

He stepped in closer and cradled her cheek with his palm. She leaned into his touch.

"I've always loved you too, Jane."

Her face lit up with the admission.

"Which is why I begged the Lord last night to help you to forgive me and to move on." He cleared his throat, but it still hurt to say. "I prayed that you could find someone worthy of you, your beauty, your love."

Scarlett straightened away from him and folded her arms across her chest. "You're an amazing, impressive man, Griff Quinn, but you're also an insensitive idiot," she flung at him.

Griff shook his head. Did he need to keep going with his rap sheet? Tell her about the many other times he'd killed innocent and not-so-innocent people? Tell her how he was going to get himself killed because of the irrational, insane way he reacted in battle?

He studied her beautiful face and couldn't do it. "Look," he ground out. "I know I've hurt you, and I can't stand to hurt you anymore. Your plan of us loving each other, while I go to do my ops and then come back to you on my off days?" He gave a disbelieving grunt. "You are the most amazing person, Scarlett. You're smart, you're beautiful, you're talented, but you truly live in a fantasy world. You have to realize someone like me in your life isn't reality. It would never work."

Her eyes glinted dangerously, and she stubbornly tilted her head. "Who are you to tell me I can't love you, I can't wait for you? I realize your job is dangerous, but it's worth the risk to be with you."

Griff pushed out a quick breath. Risking her wasn't worth it, no matter how badly he wanted to be with her. Yet she looked close to falling apart, and he couldn't stand to fight with her anymore. "Oh, Jane. C'mere." He opened his arms.

She glared at him for half a second, then threw herself against his chest. He wrapped her up tight, savoring the feel of her body against his, savoring this memory. He trailed his fingers through her soft hair and along her back. He tried to memorize the way her hands traced along his back, her acceptance of his scars, of him.

Finally, he forced himself to pull back. "I can't think of how to explain to you how much I love you."

She smiled, her green eyes soft with hope.

"And that's why I can't be with you."

"Griff Quinn!" she yelled at him. "Don't you dare do this to me again. I want to be strong for you, but I need you. You have to see that. You claim you don't want to hurt me, but you're going to rip me apart if you leave me now."

Griff's heart twisted painfully. "I should've never taken this job. You could've forgotten about me and been happy."

"That's what you don't understand." She pulled from his arms, and he let her go. "I have *never* been truly happy without you. I've lived in my make-believe world, as you call it, and I've chosen to have a good attitude and make the best of each day, but every night I've prayed that you would come back to me."

"Oh, Jane," he moaned.

"All of this ..." She gestured around the room, but he knew she meant this whole deal with the million-dollar bounty and Sutton getting the intel to protect her and sending Griff. "It had to be an answer to my prayers. It had to be." Her eyes narrowed. "Who are you to tell Him—" She pointed up. "—that He's not in charge?"

"I'm a machine," he tried to explain. "I obey orders. I infiltrate and take down and kill. I fling myself into danger. I don't even feel guilty about any of it anymore. How can you honestly tell me that the good Lord would want someone perfect like you with a monster like me? A monster who will most likely be dead tomorrow?"

Scarlett's lips thinned, but she held her ground. "How can you honestly tell me that the good Lord wouldn't want you to have a chance at redemption? He loves you, Griff. Of course He wants you to be happy."

Griff shook his head. There was no way to come to an agreement here. Her perception was completely slanted from his view. "I understand that people can be forgiven for their sins, but not if they keep returning to that sin and never forsake it."

She opened her mouth to protest, but Griff held up a hand. "I have no intention of quitting my work. I will continue to take down demented people to free the innocent, and that means I will continue to lie, cheat, steal, and kill to win against them, and eventually I'll be killed by one of them. There is no world where purity like yours can exist with filth like me."

A single tear crested Scarlett's eyelid and rolled down her cheek. She brushed it angrily away with the back of her hand. "The part you have wrong is assuming you're filthy, Griff. You're not a monster; you're not evil. Did you even listen to yourself? You're freeing the innocent, giving your life to right wrongs. That's the hero, my love." She placed her palm over his heart. "This is the heart of a hero."

Griff loved her words and her sincerity, but he couldn't internalize it any more than he could allow this to continue. He let himself look at her beautiful face for a few seconds, savor the feel of her warm palm against his chest; then he prepared himself to break her heart all over again. He stepped back, and her hand fell to her side. "We'll never see eye to eye on this. Never. You didn't listen closely to what I pray for, Scarlett. I pray for you to move on, to find happiness with another man." His voice broke as he said it, but he cleared his throat and continued. "If you truly love me, please do that. For me." It was such a twisted request, but it was the only hope he had of protecting her and keeping her far from him and his role in life.

Scarlett's eyes brightened with tears. She let out a choked sob, and then she ran around him and out of the room.

Griff stood without moving for several horrible minutes. Once again, he wanted to chase after her, but this was for the best. He said his prayer again that she'd forgive and forget and move on, but he added another request—for Sutton to find the man responsible for Scarlett's hit and take him out. This job could not last much longer. Griff couldn't handle being close to her yet not loving her.

CHAPTER EIGHTEEN

Scarlett twisted and turned on the comfortable bed. She'd think at some point she'd be so exhausted she'd sleep, but today had been even worse than yesterday. She knew Griff loved her, but he thought he was protecting her by praying that she'd move on and not be part of his world. Move on to another man. He'd really said that, and he'd gotten choked up as he said it. It was obvious he didn't really want that, but he was so selfless, so dense to how love worked and how desperately she loved him. The jerk thought moving on was the best thing for her. He wasn't a jerk, though, and she'd had that insight into part of what he'd gone through. It was horrible and she should be strong enough to let him go, but she couldn't do it.

She pounded her fists into the mattress as hot tears slid out of her eyes. She thought she'd been miserable without Griff. She was a million times more miserable with him in the next room. Maybe she was just a pathetic shell of a person. So many people claimed she was the nicest person they'd ever known, that she was independent, strong, and a role model. They didn't know who she was deep down, didn't know that inside she ached for Griff every moment of the day. Maybe Griff was right and it was time for her to pray that they could both move on. Pray that Griff would find redemption and joy in his work, and that she'd find someone else, or be happy alone. Alone sounded easier. The thought of not being with Griff jabbed into her like a hot poker.

She slipped out of bed and onto her knees, pouring out her pain, her regrets, her anguish, and her hopes and dreams. No matter what Griff said, she simply couldn't bring herself to pray that she'd move on. Instead, she prayed that somehow his heart would be softened and he would understand his worth in Heavenly Father's eyes and in hers.

"Jane!" The scream from Griff's room yanked her head off of her folded arms. Another nightmare?

She murmured a quick amen and ran for her bedroom door. If this wasn't an answer to prayers, she'd know soon enough, but she wasn't giving up on the good Lord, or on Griff. Flinging her door open, she hurried to his door, but forced herself to slow down so she wouldn't jolt him awake like she had last night. She pushed on the handle and the door. It swung silently open. Scarlett crept into the room. Griff had kicked off the covers and he was curled on his side. The light of the moon off the snow gave her enough clarity to see the deep scars on his back.

As she got closer, she heard him moan her name, and then his body shuddered. His face looked younger, but it was wracked with as much pain as she'd seen earlier today. He looked weaker than she'd ever seen him. Not that Griff could ever be weak.

Maybe vulnerable was a better word to describe him—sleeping, but not at peace. It had to mean something that in his sleep he called for her.

She placed her hand on his shoulder and whispered, "Griff."

He shot up in bed and yelled, "Jane!" His eyes were wild.

"I'm here," Scarlett tried to soothe him. She put both hands on his chest. "It's okay, Griff. I'm here."

"Oh, thank the good Lord," he grunted out. He reached up and pulled her onto his lap.

Scarlett gasped in surprise. His face was inches from hers. His eyes were still a little unfocused, but they were also hungry as they drank her in.

"I love you," he said fervently, and he pulled her in tight against him and captured her mouth with his.

Scarlett returned the kiss with all the love and passion she'd been storing up for him. Her arms wrapped around his neck and she was swept away as they savored each other, the connection that had always overwhelmed her when Griff kissed her. Griff's hands cradled her close and his mouth worked its magic. His lips were much softer than the rest of him, but he didn't take the kiss soft or easy. This was the kiss of a man who was hungry for his love, and she savored each movement of his lips, his strong body surrounding her, and his clean, fresh scent.

Scarlett didn't know how long they kissed, and she didn't care. All she cared about was Griff. Oh, how she adored this tough, hardened, and beautiful man.

He finally pulled back. His breath was ragged and his blue eyes were very, very clear. "Oh, Scarlett. I shouldn't have."

"Don't you dare, Griff Quinn." She shook a finger at him. "Don't you dare regret that kiss, or I'll ... punch my fist down *your* throat."

Griff's eyes widened; then he chuckled. He sobered and his eyes tenderly roved over her face, a gentle caress so full of love it made her quiver. "Ah, Jane. Why do you make this so tough?"

She brought her palms along his neck and to his chest, savoring the muscle under her fingertips. Griff let out a soft moan, and she loved it. "You're the one making this tough. Just kiss me, Griff."

Griff swallowed hard and stared at her. She could feel the quick thrum of his heartbeat under her right palm, and she knew her heart was going even faster. He tenderly framed her face with his hands, and she ran her hands over his shoulders and down to his biceps.

"Yes, ma'am," he murmured, and then he was kissing her again. Rational thought disappeared, but Scarlett did find herself hoping he didn't think this was tough or she really would punch him, see how hard those lovely abs of his really were. She clung to his biceps and he trailed his hands along her cheeks and into her hair. The kiss continued with the perfect amount of pressure from Griff's mouth, and the nerve endings in her lips were all lit up with the pleasure and sheer joy of it.

Griff was the first one to break away—of course. He scooted back, resting his back against the pillows and headboard, and he gently lifted her off his lap and next to him on the bed. He wrapped one arm around her lower back and cupped her cheek with his other hand, pulling her head down to his chest and simply cradling her close.

Scarlett loved laying her head against his chest, feeling the warm flesh, hearing his heartbeat, but she was scared right now. Griff hadn't pushed her away, but she knew he wasn't going to just soften and agree to be with her because he'd said he loved her and they'd shared some unreal kisses.

When she could take it no longer, she pulled back slightly and looked up at him. His hand fell down to cup her hip. His face was much too serious.

"What are you thinking?" she forced herself to ask.

Griff tilted his head toward her. "I'm thinking how beautiful you are."

Scarlett smiled, waiting for him to shatter the moment.

"And I'm thinking how stupid I've been to not have spent the last four days kissing you."

Scarlett laughed, but inside she knew the ball was going to drop and she'd have to fight for the ground she'd just gained.

"You don't agree?" he asked, arching an eyebrow at her.

"I've been begging you to kiss me since you came to my house that first night."

"You have?" His eyes filled with wonder.

"I don't want to call you an idiot again, but you are horrific at picking up on nonverbal cues."

Griff laughed. "I don't think any person has dared call me an idiot, a jerk, or stupid before."

"I'm sure they thought it." She winked. "Why do you let me get away with it?"

His gaze deepened. "You should know. You're the only person I love this deeply." Griff lifted her back onto his lap, and she wrapped her arms around his neck again. "I thought it would be smarter to not let myself kiss you like I've been dreaming of." His breath was coming hard and fast. "But apparently tonight I am an idiot."

Scarlett smiled. "As long as you're an idiot for me."

"Always, Jane." He tugged her tight and proceeded to tell her with his lips what he'd never fully conveyed with words—he adored her, he'd give anything for her, and she was the only woman he'd ever loved. His lips were warm and thirsty, and he did not kiss her slow and languidly. He kissed her like a man who had been longing for her for many years. She matched his need with a growing desire of her own. She was the first one to deepen the kiss, and he let out a soft moan before making her mouth tingle as he returned the action.

When he pulled back, he tenderly kissed her jaw, then her neck. His lips lingered there. "I've missed your neck," he breathed into her skin.

Scarlett framed his face and pulled him up level with her. "More than my lips?"

Griff gave her a slow grin, his eyes smoldering with desire for her. "It's a toss-up."

"Jerk."

"I am."

Scarlett smiled and waited for him to kiss her again. She moistened her lips and ran her thumbs along his jaw, savoring being so close to him, and she waited.

Griff leaned away from her instead. "Aw, Jane, I am such a jerk."

"What?" *No, no, no!*

"I can't be kissing you, loving you, when I know I'll leave you again." His arms loosened around her, but at least he didn't push her away. "This is what I've been trying to avoid ... hurting you more. If you'd never discovered how much I still love you, wouldn't it be easier when I disappear from your life again?"

Scarlett's heart thudded painfully. She wanted to beg him to not disappear, but she knew that wasn't reality. She'd had quite the crash course in reality since Griff Quinn reappeared in her life. Reality stunk, and it hurt, but it was also beautiful. Griff was beautiful, no matter that he'd scoff if she said that. Loving him was hard but beautiful to her. She wasn't truly real with anyone in her life, except him. She was real with Griff, and he was real to her.

"I'm calling a truce, a cease-fire, waving the white flag," she said.

Griff stared at her like she was delusional.

"I'm done with the battle, Griff. I can't convince you how perfectly wonderful you are to me, and you can't convince me that we'll never be together. So we can either be miserable and fight about it, or we can dump the battle and savor what time we have."

Griff's eyes widened. "But what about when I have to leave you?"

Scarlett kissed him softly. "Then I'll pray you can come back to me."

Griff's chest heaved with emotion. He pulled her in tighter and whispered against her forehead, "I love you so much, Jane, but I'm still terrified that you're living in a fantasy world, that you don't understand what or who I am."

"You're the man I love, Griff. That's all that matters to me."

Griff kissed her passionately, and by the time he released her, she was hearing wedding bells and seeing him in a tux. She knew that might never be reality, so she forced herself to stay in the moment.

"What do you want from me?" he asked in a rough voice. If Scarlett didn't know him better, she'd think he was tearing up.

"I just want you," she said.

"What if you can't have me?"

Scarlett looked up at him. "I have you right now, Griff. That's all that matters. Just hold me tonight and we'll take it one day at a time. As long as you don't shut me out or give up on us again, we can make it through anything."

"Even death?"

His eyes were scared. She knew he'd seen many deaths. Scarlett had never seen death in real life. What she wouldn't give to take his pain and memories away.

She lifted herself closer and cradled his handsome face in her hands. "Even death, my love. This world isn't the end, and if one of us gets left behind, don't you want to have these memories of being together until we can be reunited in heaven?"

Griff simply stared at her. He didn't scoff or disagree, but he didn't agree either. Instead he carefully lifted her onto the bed next to him and laid her on her back. He then slid down next to her and cradled her against his chest. "I love you, Jane," he whispered gruffly.

"I love you, Griff."

She lay there in the circle of his arms, one hand on his chest, savoring the connection with him. Griff loved her. He'd always protect her, and he wanted to be there for her, but he couldn't promise that.

They were at an uneasy cease-fire, where he could retreat from her emotionally at any moment. They might never come to terms and end the battle, but tonight she was going to enjoy being close to him. She wouldn't spoil it by thinking about what tomorrow might bring. She knew that all too soon he would leave her again, physically if not emotionally. There was no way to avoid it, no matter what either of them wanted.

CHAPTER NINETEEN

Griff had another crappy night's sleep, but he couldn't have cared less. He'd held Scarlett throughout the long, beautiful night, her lovely form pressed close to him, her soft hair tickling his chest. He'd loved every minute of it.

Now the sun was peeking over the mountains and glaring through the windows. He smiled as he thought of Scarlett worrying about him not being able to handle too much sunshine, asking if that's why he didn't want her. He'd told her he wanted her plenty, and that was the truth. He gazed down at her beautiful face, peaceful in sleep. He wanted her more than anything in this world, but she was right about their battle. While a ceasefire was a nice idea, it couldn't last when neither party could see where the other was coming from. She talked bravely about death, but had she seen death in real life, off the movie screen? He doubted it, or she wouldn't be so brave.

He closed his eyes, and horrific images resurfaced. People claimed he was brave. He'd definitely done his share of brave, and stupid, jobs for the SEALs and for Sutton, but inside he wasn't brave at all. He was terrified to die, terrified to leave his family and Scarlett, and terrified to face his Maker and atone for the atrocities he'd committed. Yet he still plunged into battle every chance he got. It must be ingrained in his soul. His reaction was to fight and protect, and he'd never withdrawn from the battle or the consequences, for anyone or any reason.

Scarlett shifted and let out the cutest little moan. Griff was brought back to the beautiful reality of having her next to him. She was right about one thing—they should savor this time, because the dream of them spending their lives together, having children, growing old and gray? That was an impossible dream.

Her eyelashes fluttered, and then those green eyes that he loved so much were staring up at him. "Morning, handsome," she murmured.

"Morning, beautiful."

"What fun adventures do you have planned for us today—snowmobile ride, *Just Dance* competition, fighting with wolves?" She arched a delicate eyebrow.

Griff wanted to kiss her all day. Instead he released her, climbed off the bed, and offered her a hand. Scarlett placed her hand in his, and he helped her to her feet. "How about we work out and then make breakfast together?"

"Ah, the safe choice—you couldn't keep up with me snowmobiling or dancing, and the wolves are too scared of us to come back." She squeezed his hand and grinned.

Griff chuckled. "All true."

She released his hand and turned as if to go, but she stopped. "We're still at white flag status, correct?" She looked up at him, so appealing that he could hardly resist kissing her.

He nodded.

The relief in her eyes made him realize all over again how much he'd hurt her for so many years. Guilt made his stomach churn.

"How long can two parties with differing views stay at a truce?" she asked.

Griff shrugged. "Forty to fifty years?" It was the wrong thing to say. He couldn't lead her on for forty to fifty years, but he'd never live that long, so it wasn't really worth worrying about.

Scarlett hugged him quickly, then skipped to the door like an adorable little girl. No, that was the wrong description; no little girl could look that irresistible in yoga pants and a T-shirt. She tossed a wink over her shoulder before hurrying to her room.

Griff found a clean T-shirt and put on socks and shoes. He brushed his teeth, applied some deodorant, and exited his room to wait outside Scarlett's. She came out wearing the same T-shirt from last night, some shorts, and the socks and shoes he'd bought her at Wal-Mart. Her long, blonde hair was tied up in a ponytail.

Griff reached for her and pulled her in tight. He bowed down low to kiss the soft skin of her neck. Scarlett giggled and pulled his face up to hers. "My lips are up here."

"Ah, I usually never miss."

She laughed, but he cut it off as he pressed his lips to hers. He pressed her against the wall and took his time kissing her. There was no rush, and they were in their own world. When he pulled back, her chest was rising and falling quickly.

"I forgot. We're supposed to work out." He arched an eyebrow playfully.

"This is getting my heart beating plenty. But I know what gets your heart beating." She feathered her fingers along his abdomen.

Griff started laughing immediately. He used to hate that he was ticklish, but with Scarlett around, it was pure pleasure. He grabbed her hand and held it tight. "Stop."

"Or what?" She stared up at him, so innocent and beautiful.

"Or I'll kiss you."

Her eyes twinkled. "Oh, the threats."

He pulled her off her feet and against his chest and kissed her. It was a long time before they got to the basement to exercise. Griff had been involved in cease-fires and truces before. They'd never come close to the joy of Scarlett in his arms.

Scarlett loved working out with Griff close by. They teased and taunted each other to run faster on the treadmill or lift heavier weights. She could almost keep up with his running speed, but she couldn't come within a quarter of the amount of weight he could lift.

This truce they had agreed upon, or rather she'd forced on him, was like stolen, precious moments for her. She knew he was serious that he'd have to leave her again, but she was serious that she'd wait and that he was more than worthy of a relationship with her.

As he did an overhead press, he caught her gaze in the mirror. His blue eyes filled with warmth and desire for her. How she loved this man.

"Remember when we used to work out together in college?" she asked.

He grinned. "Yeah. I could out-lift you then, too."

She laughed. "You weigh twice what I do, so it's not that impressive you can lift twice as much." He was so impressive that she couldn't tear her eyes away from him, but there was no reason to inflate his ego.

"Hmm." He shelved the eighty-pound dumbbells. "So I just did an overhead press with eighty-pounders, and you did it with ...?" He looked at the weights still in her hands. "Fifteen?" He nodded. "Double?"

Scarlett simply laughed and re-shelved her weights. "But I also remember in college you never lifted weights with a shirt on." She arched an eyebrow. It was silly of her to bring it up, but she would love, love, love to watch all the muscles in his upper body work in synchrony.

His smile kind of froze, but he said, "In college, I was just trying to impress you."

"And you're not trying to impress me now?"

"You've made it more than obvious you want me now." He winked and walked over to the cable machine.

Scarlett followed him. She put her hands at his waist, fingering the bottom of his T-shirt. Griff froze. She went on tiptoes, leaned against him, and whispered close to his right ear. "Your back is every bit as attractive to me now as it was in college."

Griff didn't move. Scarlett lowered onto her heels, leaned back, and ran her fingertips up under his T-shirt. She trailed her fingers and palms over the bumpy skin of his back, savoring the well-developed muscles underneath and the connection to this amazing man.

Griff turned slowly to face her, and Scarlett's hands stopped on his waist. He looked slowly over her face, and then he put his hands on her upper arms and pulled her closer. "Thank you," he whispered.

"For?"

"Loving me."

"It's what I was born to do."

Griff smiled at that and bent down, tenderly kissing her. Scarlett ran her hands up under his T-shirt and held on to his broad back. His scars only made him more tough, real, and incredible to her. She savored his kiss and this tender side of the man she loved. She was afraid that all too soon the warrior would reappear and shut himself off from her again.

For the first time in five days, she prayed that the man who'd offered a million dollars for her would never be found and she and Griff would have to hide in this cabin indefinitely. If Griff knew her prayer, he'd tease her that she was living in a dream world. She didn't care what world she was living in, as long as Griff was with her.

After a long workout, they'd eaten a quick breakfast of yogurt parfaits—with a side of six scrambled eggs for Griff—then gone upstairs to shower. It was hard to break away from Scarlett, even to take a shower, but Griff wanted to be clean and get his teeth freshly brushed. His plan for today was to show her he could dance to that Wii thing and then watch a movie while he held her, sneaking in kisses every chance he got. He was certain if his family members and SEAL brothers were watching him right now, they would guess that an imposter had taken over his body, or that Scarlett had bewitched him. He was pretty sure the latter was true.

He remembered Jasmine telling him to kiss Scarlett. Smiling, he thought that Jasmine would be happy at how sappy he was being, but she would also laugh until her stomach hurt. Thinking of Jasmine made him realize that somehow she and Kaleb made it work. Now that she could possibly be recognized as Kaleb Quinn's wife, Sutton was very careful what missions he sent her on and she always had an altered appearance.

Yet the ops that his sister-in-law was involved in were as dangerous as Griff's, sometimes more so. Quite often she dressed up like a desperate college student, went to bars where young women had disappeared, and allowed herself to be kidnapped, then took down a trafficking ring from the inside while Griff and other of Sutton's men dismantled it from the outside. Somehow Kaleb dealt with his wife being in dangerous, horrific situations. Would Scarlett be able to do the same?

He heard a rap on his door and he hurried to it, swinging it open. Scarlett smiled brightly at him, her long hair dark blonde with wetness and her face clean and so beautiful. He didn't waste any time, quickly tugging her against his chest. Bending down, he kissed her and then inhaled deeply. "Thanks for using the peaches-and-cream stuff."

She laughed. "That was pretty cute of you to buy it."

"Cute?" Griff scoffed. "You realize you can't tell anybody that I'm cute, soft, or absolutely, insanely crazy about you."

Scarlett's smile lit up her green eyes. "Sorry. I'm already planning the press conference I'm going to have after I get back home. The whole world will know the fearsome Griff Quinn is nobody to be afraid of."

Griff gave her a stern glare, though he felt so happy and light inside that he almost didn't know how to deal with these foreign emotions. "Then I'm afraid I'm going to have to silence you."

"Oh, really? And how do you plan to do that?"

Griff shrugged. "Remember you left me no choice." He picked her up, spun her around, and held her against the wall. She gasped out, and he laughed, then proceeded to kiss her until they were both panting for air.

When he finally lowered her feet to the ground, he trailed his hands along her neck and smiled as she trembled under his touch. "Sworn to silence now, right?"

"Not even close, Mr. Quinn. You'll have to 'silence me' daily if you don't want the truth to come out."

"Gladly." He pinned her against the wall with both hands, bowed his head, and started with her soft neck and then worked his way up to her lips.

His phone buzzed in his pocket. He groaned and released her, pulling it out. Sutton. His gaze darted to her. Sutton had sent some texts about their progress and the leads they'd found, but he wouldn't be calling unless ...

Scarlett blinked up at him. "You okay?"

"I ... yes." He stepped back and slid his finger across the screen. "Sir?"

"We got him."

Griff faltered for a response. This was great news, fabulous news. His gaze met Scarlett's. This news meant their time together was over. She'd promised to wait for him, but he could be on another job by tomorrow. The thought of being away from her for even a minute made his shoulders round.

"Was it the mafia leader from Columbia?" Griff asked.

"Yeah. Guess he was enamored with her, wanted to marry her. He's a huge drug trafficker as well, so we killed two birds with one bullet, so to speak."

The guy was dead. Griff was relieved ... and he hated to have this time with Scarlett at an end.

She didn't move, searching his face for answers.

"I'm sending my Cessna for Scarlett. She'll have some time to relax this afternoon before she deals with the press tomorrow. Why don't you get moving and meet the pilot in Salt Lake? It's a little slower than my Airbus, so it should take you both about four hours to get there. I'll send you the coordinates to the commuter airport. Do you mind driving the Escalade back here?"

"Not at all, sir." Ten hours on the road without Scarlett would be miserable, but Griff had been the soldier for so long that saying no to his superior wasn't even a possibility.

"Good work, Griff."

"Thank you, sir. You too." Griff hadn't done good work. Yes, he'd protected Scarlett, but he'd lost his heart to her in the process, and now he was going to have to break them both into pieces when he left for his next op.

"Heart of a warrior," said Sutton, signing off.

"Heart of a warrior," Griff repeated. He slid the phone into his pocket, shoved one hand through his short hair, and stared down at Scarlett.

"Hey," she whispered. She lifted her hand and massaged at the furrow that had probably appeared between his brows. "Why are you looking all moody and broody over there?"

Griff forced a smile, captured her hand with his, and placed a lingering kiss in her palm. "Great news, actually."

"Oh? Then why are you frowning?"

Was he still frowning? Was the anguish over losing her again coming through? "They found the guy."

"That offered the money for me?"

He nodded and kept the fake smile on his face, which took more of a concerted effort than battling three men at once. "So it's over. Sutton's sending his plane for you. We need to meet him in Salt Lake City, which is about four hours from here, so we'd better get moving." He stepped back and turned to go to his room. They'd kept the house clean during their stay, but he'd still try to pay for Tucker's cleaning crew. That would be a battle.

Battle. He stopped and focused on Scarlett. She didn't want to battle with him; these hours of cease-fire had been some of the best of his life. She truly loved him, no matter what he'd done, what he'd become. How was she going to cope when he disappeared from her life?

"You okay?" he asked.

Her green eyes were filled with concern. "I don't want to say goodbye."

"Ah, Jane." He gathered her into his arms and simply held her. They'd see each other soon in California, but it would probably only be days before Sutton needed him on a new assignment. Would it be goodbye then? She was probably waiting for him to promise it wouldn't be goodbye, but Griff only lied to criminals. He couldn't lie to her, even if it would make her feel better.

CHAPTER TWENTY

Scarlett kept Griff talking through the drive to Salt Lake City. Nothing deep, mostly about his family and the experiences she'd had since they'd been apart. He didn't share much about what he'd done the past ten years. She imagined some of it he legally couldn't share and much of it he didn't want to share.

When they reached the small commuter airport in Salt Lake, the plane was waiting for them. The wind was blowing, and it chilled Scarlett clear through. The good thing about Sutton Smith taking out the guy who'd offered money for her was she'd get back to California and warm weather. The bad thing ... She stared up at Griff's handsome face. Being away from Griff was the bad thing and it was horrible to contemplate that separation.

The pilot shook their hands, looking a little wide-eyed to be meeting Scarlett Lily. He gestured into the plane. "This way, Miss Lily. We'll get you home safe, ma'am."

"Thank you." She turned to Griff. "I don't want to leave you for a minute," she burst out. It was very thoughtful of Sutton to send his plane so she could have more time to decompress before facing everybody tomorrow, mostly the media, but she wished Griff would've told him not to send it.

Griff gave her a soft smile and an even softer kiss. "I'll drive straight through and meet you at your house a few hours after you get there."

Scarlett's heart beat faster. All she wanted was more time with Griff. Why did it feel like stolen time? She ignored the pilot, who was staring at the two of them. "Don't drive straight through. You need some sleep or you'll probably kill yourself."

"Do you realize how highly trained I am, ma'am? I'll be wide awake thinking about being with you again."

Scarlett wrapped her arms around his neck and clung to him. The brisk wind stung her back, but Griff held her close and she could stand out here for hours if it meant being in his arms.

Griff pulled back and gently tugged her arms from around his neck. "It's okay, love. I'll see you soon."

"You promise?" She hated that her eyes pricked with unshed tears. She didn't want to be weak. She wanted to be strong, strong enough to stand by this man's side.

"I promise." His blue eyes were somber yet filled with a light she hadn't seen in them five days ago. He loved her, and he had hope they could make it work. She knew it.

She kissed him quickly, pulled back, and ran up the short set of stairs to the plane. The pilot followed her on and asked her to please choose any seat. Scarlett glanced back out the still-open door. Griff stood there, looking so strong and irresistible. He grinned at her and lifted a hand. The pilot closed the door. Scarlett felt like her body was being ripped apart by one of those wolves. Griff would see her soon and she was being dramatic and silly. She had to be strong. If knowing she'd be apart from Griff for ten hours was killing her like this, how would she deal with him leaving for an op that took months?

She buckled up and looked out the window. Griff stood next to the Escalade. He saw her watching him and smiled, inclining his chin to her. She made a heart with her hands and put it up so he could see it. Griff's smile grew and he returned the gesture. Scarlett wished she could take a picture. She wouldn't tell the world how soft he was for her like she'd teased him about, but she'd savor the memory of it when she had to be apart from him.

CHAPTER TWENTY-ONE

Scarlett was exhausted when she finally walked into her house. It was early evening. She should've slept on the plane, but every time she drifted off, she'd remember something Griff said, or did. She loved him so much, and it was a lot more fun to savor memories of him than sleep.

Sutton was waiting for her at the airport and drove her to her house. He explained how they'd found the mafia leader, Gilberto Rodriguez, at his home in Columbia, and the man admitted he'd put the million-dollar bounty on her head because he wanted her for his wife. Rodriguez's men had initiated a shoot-out and the man had been killed. It was such a relief. Sutton had also cleared everything with the police so her home was no longer being watched by them. She'd have to get with her agent in the morning and work on damage control from all the media.

When she got home, she immediately showered and put on some of her own clothes, a comfy tank top and skirt. It felt good to use her own toiletries and wear her own clothes, but she would miss the clothes Griff had bought her, and she'd miss smelling like peaches and cream. She smiled as she fingered her blonde locks and looked at herself in the mirror. She was going to stay blonde. Nobody would be happy about it, except Griff. His was the only opinion that mattered to her.

She tilted open the blinds in her bedroom suite and stared out at the view of the ocean. How many more hours until Griff would be here? Maybe only an hour or two if he'd truly driven straight through. She kept praying that he'd be safe and would stop to sleep if he got too tired. She wanted him close, but she wanted him safe more.

The sun sank into the ocean as she stared at the view. Scarlett simply enjoyed the beautiful sight, in no real hurry. At least, not until Griff got here. Then she'd be in a hurry to kiss him and make the most of each moment they had.

Walking downstairs, she debated what to make for dinner. The food in her fridge was probably all moldy, and she wasn't calling her chef or personal shopper tonight. She wasn't up to answering any questions.

She was almost to the bottom step when she heard soft breathing. Fear rushed through her, and Scarlett pivoted to run back up the stairs. From behind her, two men grabbed her by the arms and yanked her off the stairs and into the living area.

A handsome, polished-looking man with black hair and smooth skin stood there, grinning at her. "My Scarlett Lily," he said. "Finally, I find you."

"Who are you?" she asked, trying to break the men's hold. Her heart was racing out of control, and cold sweat pricked at her neck. Griff! He was too far away to come for her.

"Gilberto Rodriguez." He gave her a toothy grin. "And you, Scarlett Lily, have the honor of being my queen."

"Sutton killed you," she gasped out. This was the man who had offered a million dollars for her? What would he do with her now? How was he not dead?

"Ah, Sutton Smith. Very smart of you to involve the enigma in your protection. But I outsmarted him. My double has been at my home, waiting for Sutton Smith's men to arrive, since I put the million-dollar reward out for you."

Scarlett's jaw dropped and she was sure she looked like a caricature with her eyes wide. This man had outsmarted Sutton and Griff.

"I am too smart for any of the American cowboys. I have hidden funds worth hundreds of millions of dollars, and you and I will spend as many years as we want on a private island that no one knows I own. I will have to manage my affairs in Columbia, but I can do that all remotely. The million-dollar bounty didn't work out because you disappeared so quickly, but I knew as soon as my double was killed you'd reappear. Coming personally for you was more work than I wanted, but you're worth it, and I know you'll make it up to me." He leered at her. "So, my love, are you ready to go fulfill your destiny?"

Scarlett let out a disbelieving grunt. "No," she said shortly. "I am not your queen, and I'm going nowhere with you."

"I'm sorry, love, but I've always known you were meant for me. You've been in my future, simply waiting for me to come for you." He spread his hands benevolently and his smile never left his face, though his dark eyes were chillier than the wind in Island Park. He snapped his fingers. "Let's go." He walked through her living area and kitchen toward her mudroom.

Scarlett struggled to free herself, twisting and pulling. She didn't think they'd kill her after doing so much to kidnap her so she tried to delay them taking her away. Fighting with everything in her the men struggled to gain control of her flailing limbs. When they almost had her pinned, she dropped to the ground and tried to yank free, but the men lifted her up, pinned her between them, and hurried after their boss.

Terror made her stomach churn. Would Griff be able to find her? If anyone could, Griff could, but how could she leave him a trail to follow when she didn't know where they were taking her? Would her security cameras pick something up? She'd always felt so safe in her house, but these men had bypassed her security just like that other man and Griff had days ago. It seemed years had passed since Griff had reappeared in her life.

They dragged her through her garage and out a side entrance. Normally exterior lights lit up this area, but the spot was dark. She could hear the waves crashing on the beach below her house, but no sounds of a vehicle or help approaching. If she somehow escaped this Gilberto creeper, she was definitely changing security companies.

"Help!" she screamed, praying someone would be walking on the beach or the security who kept failing her would be making the rounds of the neighborhood. "Hel—" Her second scream was cut off as one of the men clamped his hand over her mouth.

"Mario? Carlos?" Gilberto's harsh whisper came from the bushes next to her house.

Scarlett's captors stopped, pinning her tightly. She squinted to make Gilberto out in the dark and finally could see him bent low over two prostrate bodies.

Her fear increased, but then she realized that if those were Gilberto's men, maybe help had come. She tried to scream again, but the man's hand was too tight over her mouth.

A large black shadow appeared behind Gilberto and drove an elbow between the mafia lord's shoulder blades, and he flattened on top of his men without much more than a "whump."

The man straightened, and Scarlett peered into the darkness. "Let her go and I might let you live," his gruff voice said.

Griff! Happiness and hope made her feel light, even though the men hadn't released her.

One man shoved her against the other. He leveled his gun on Griff. Griff flew straight at him.

"No!" Scarlett yelled as she strained against her captor. Using the man as leverage, she jumped and kicked the other man's hand. Her foot connected with flesh. The pistol went off.

Griff rammed into the guy and knocked him to the ground. He pounded his fists into the man's face until the guy was limp.

The man holding Scarlett clasped her tighter, one arm around her neck, one around her shoulder. Griff stood slowly, looking like the toughest hero she'd ever seen. His muscles rippled and he was the perfect mix of serious and protective. It was obvious he was going to thump this guy, and it was obvious he loved Scarlett.

The psycho mafia guy was still holding her tight. He was close to her height, but much stronger than her. She couldn't budge in his grip.

Griff focused in on the guy. "Let her go," he said in a steely tone.

"I break her neck," the man muttered. He grasped her chin with one hand and her shoulder with the other.

"No!" Griff roared, throwing himself at them.

Scarlett's stomach plunged with horror, but she had been in too many action shows to not know what to do. She brought her heel up, hard, and it landed right between the man's legs. His grip on her faltered as he howled in pain. She slipped to the ground and rolled away just as Griff barreled into the guy. The man's head slammed against the concrete and he went still immediately.

Griff jumped off of him and whirled to her. "Scarlett?" His voice was shaky and smaller than she'd ever heard.

"I'm okay," she managed, pushing to her feet.

She hadn't even stood before Griff was scooping her up and into his arms. "Oh, love, oh, Jane," he kept repeating over and over as he tenderly held her as if she would break.

A few vehicles raced up to the house and men popped out of them. Scarlett clung to Griff, praying these weren't more of the mafia guys. Yet Griff could best anyone, so she didn't know why she even worried.

The men, and one small woman, strode up to the house. Scarlett recognized Sutton Smith and Jasmine, Griff's sister-in-law. Sutton's men started checking the men on the ground. Sutton strode up and reached out to the two of them. Griff set her on her feet and kept one arm around her as she and Griff each shook Sutton's hand.

"See why you were the ace for this job?" Sutton asked, tilting his head toward the men Griff had dismantled.

"The other Gilberto was a phony," Griff said.

"Looks like it," Sutton agreed.

"How did you get here so fast? How did you know something was wrong?" Scarlett asked Griff.

"I drove twenty miles over the speed limit the whole way," Griff said.

"Just wanted to be with me?"

Griff bent and kissed her. "Yes, love, I did."

Jasmine whistled long and low, but they both ignored her.

"But how did you know something was wrong?" Scarlett asked. "You'd already taken those two men out before we came outside."

"When I pulled up, I noticed the exterior lights were out on that side of the house. I parked in your neighbor's driveway and worked my way around the back of the house until I found them. Then I sent a message to Sutton before taking them out."

"You're the perfect hero." Scarlett grabbed Griff's shirt, pulled him close, and kissed him firmly on the lips in front of everyone.

Griff smiled. "I just want to be your hero, love."

"Who are you and what have you done with my brother-in-law?" Jasmine asked.

Griff cast a quick, concerned glance toward Sutton.

Sutton returned the look with raised brows and a half smile. "Knew her a long time ago, eh?"

Griff lifted his shoulders, cuddling Scarlett closer.

Scarlett's insides felt all lit up. She kissed Griff again, ignoring the faint wails of sirens that were obviously heading their way, Sutton, Jasmine, or the other men watching. Griff held her in his beautiful arms, but she felt warm liquid oozing down onto her arm. She yanked back from his kiss. "Griff, your arm!"

He shrugged. "I thought you liked my scars."

Scarlett laughed, which was crazy, considering that Griff was bleeding from a bullet wound. "I love every bit of you, Griff Quinn." She turned to Sutton for help. "Sutton, he's been shot."

"It's no big deal," Griff insisted.

Sutton and Jasmine moved in close to check out Griff's wound as police converged on the house. She tried to stay close to him, but the police had to separate them for questioning and the EMTs had to check his wound, which luckily was just a graze.

Griff declined stitches and asked for Steri-Strips, winking at her. She glanced down at her arm that still had the Steri-Strips on it. The wolf scratches hadn't even bothered her. But something was really bothering her right now. If she hadn't kicked at the guy with the gun, Griff would most likely be dead. The thought made her stomach tumble. He was such a brave hero, but possibly too brave.

Despite the warm breeze, she felt a sudden chill and wrapped her arms around herself. A split second—that was all that stood between Griff taking a bullet through his arm or his heart. She could picture him motionless. The next time he put himself in a bullet's path, who would be there to protect him? How many times would his luck hold out? That's all it was—stupid, dumb luck.

Griff was brave and strong and smart and fierce, but so were the bad guys of the world. And, unlike in her movies, good didn't always triumph over evil. Could she really live with the knowledge he might be brutally taken at any time?

She glanced over at Griff, still protesting as the paramedics fussed over him. He turned toward her and flashed one of his heartbreaking smiles. Could she live in a world without him?

CHAPTER TWENTY-TWO

The EMTs finished with Griff, leaving him free to focus on Scarlett. She'd been so brave, kicking that guy who would've shot him, and then planting her heel in the crotch of the guy who would've broken her neck. Fear raced through him, and he didn't think he could handle seeing her in danger ever again. Jasmine had had a lot of issues with the worry over her past bringing danger to Kaleb. It was a valid concern for Griff and Scarlett too.

She smiled at him, and his heartbeat quickened. He would protect her. It was the only option. The EMT said he was clear to go. Griff started toward Scarlett, who was now talking with Jasmine. He'd better make sure Jasmine didn't tell her any embarrassing family secrets. Jasmine was almost as bad as Navy at trying to embarrass him. Normally he couldn't care less, but he wanted Scarlett to keep thinking he was her personal hero.

"Griff." Sutton was at his elbow.

Griff halted and turned to his boss. The respect he felt for this man was equal to the respect he felt for his own family and his SEAL brothers who had died for him. "Yes, sir?"

Sutton kept looking at him, his eyes deadly serious.

Griff's stomach turned. "What's wrong?"

"I need you in Peru ... now."

"Peru?" No! His entire body revolted at the thought of leaving Scarlett. He knew it would happen eventually, had tried to prepare her for it, but not so soon. Couldn't he have even a few days to love her before he left her? What if the next bullet aimed his way took his life? What if this undercover job was the one where he didn't play his precarious part correctly and he was slaughtered?

"The refugees from Venezuela have been pouring into Peru for a while now. Almost half a million."

Griff nodded. He knew all of this.

"The traffickers have found them in unprotected locations. They arrive with buses and tell the refugees they're taking them to a safe place with food and shelter. They're sweeping up entire families, separating and enslaving them all."

This was one of the things Griff specialized in. How could he say that he wouldn't help free hundreds of innocent and vulnerable people to be with one irresistible woman? Saving lives was what he did, and he did it well. He shouldn't even be tempted to forget his mission in life so he could hold and kiss Scarlett. He glanced her direction. Tempted he was. She was staring at him, and when he met her gaze, her green eyes filled with adoration and her lips lifted in a welcoming smile.

"I know it'll be hard to leave her," Sutton murmured. "But this is what you were made for, son."

Griff straightened his shoulders and faced his boss. "She knows who I am, sir."

Sutton nodded. "It's never easy to live our calling if you truly love someone."

Griff knew Sutton understood. He didn't hold himself above his men, and he was often in dangerous situations. His wife, Liz, was supportive, and they loved each other, but as far as Griff knew, Liz had never asked him to stop saving lives, no matter if it risked his own.

"Thank you for understanding, sir. When do I leave?"

"You've got five minutes." He turned and strode toward one of the waiting Escalades.

Griff didn't waste precious minutes watching him go. He turned to Scarlett. She was so beautiful, and he loved her. The next five minutes would push his sense of duty to the limit.

Scarlett waited with Jasmine for Griff. His sister-in-law was animatedly telling her that she'd never seen Griff so much as look longingly at a woman, and here he was, head over heels for Scarlett. She smiled and listened, but she couldn't take her eyes off Griff. When she saw him and Sutton talking so seriously and then Griff square his shoulders, her stomach plunged. He was leaving her. She knew it as surely as she knew that she loved him.

Griff strode up to them, picked her off her feet, and held her close against him. He kissed her long and hard. Scarlett loved every second of it, but it just reaffirmed her fears.

"*Excuse* me," Jasmine quipped beside them.

"You're excused," Griff said breathily, his entire focus on Scarlett.

Jasmine chuckled and slipped away from them. Griff released Scarlett, took her hand, and led her around to the back of her house. The soft patio lights showed that his jaw was set in a hard line. The breaking of the waves on the shore usually calmed Scarlett. Not right now.

Griff stopped and turned to face her. His gaze swept over her. "Have I told you how much I love you?" he asked.

"Not for at least a minute." She smiled bravely.

Griff bent low and tenderly brushed his lips over hers. It was achingly sweet.

She wanted more and she wanted it now, but she had to know. "How soon are you leaving?" she whispered.

Griff froze, staring intently into her eyes. Then he straightened and she could see his military shutter go over his face. He was distancing himself from her. She understood. He had to, or this would be too excruciating. If only she had a military shutter ... but no, she had nothing but a heart that felt ready to shatter.

No, that wasn't true. She had her actor's shutter, her make-believe world. She had to act like she was strong. For Griff.

"Sutton gave me five minutes."

She appreciated his honesty. "Where are you going?"

"Peru. To rescue refugees from the traffickers."

"Thank you for being the hero." She forced a brilliant smile and fell into the role to protect herself. She'd played this part several times, the woman sending her man off to battle. She'd been strong onscreen when her man wasn't going to make a difference in hundreds of peoples' lives; somehow she'd be strong now. But her characters had never loved any man like she loved Griff.

Griff's shutter slipped and he wrapped his arms around her and groaned. "When I shut you out of my life years ago …"

Scarlett glanced sharply up at him. This was the one place they hadn't gone and he quickly ripped through any barriers she'd tried to erect with his honesty. Griff was the real thing and even if he put his military shutter back on she would allow herself to be vulnerable for him. No more fantasy world. She only wanted Griff. No matter how hard their journey might be.

"It had nothing to do with you." He stared down at her, begging her to understand. "I earned a reputation for being invincible, or at least thinking I was. I realized early on in the military that I react differently than most men." He paused, and his eyes swept over her face. "You'd think with someone as amazing as you waiting for me, I'd understand to be cautious. But when a battle starts, I don't think—I act." He swallowed and admitted, "And my action is always to fling myself into danger."

Scarlett's body started trembling. She'd seen what he was describing earlier tonight. "When you leapt at that man with the gun tonight."

He stiffened against her. "Yeah. He would've shot me if you hadn't kicked him." His smile looked as forced as hers had felt a few seconds ago. "Thank you."

"How many times have you been shot?" she whispered.

"Only three—well, four, including tonight—but this ..." He tilted his head to his arm. "... was nothing." Griff wrapped his hands around her arms and leaned back. "We're wasting our five minutes. I just want to be kissing you."

Scarlett smiled sadly. "But you'd be avoiding the tough subject."

He eyed her warily.

"So you broke up with me after college because you were pretty sure you'd be killed soon."

He paused and then finally nodded.

"And now you're leaving." She took a slow breath and asked, "Are you planning on dying on this op?"

Griff pulled her against him and rocked her gently side to side. "I'm never planning on dying. I just wanted to explain that I don't mean to react recklessly, but it happens—often." He bent and claimed her lips with his own. It was a kiss full of passion and desperate need. A kiss that said he might not be coming back to her. He pulled back and smiled sadly down at her. "But now I have the most important reason of all to stay safe—you."

She reached up and framed his face with her hands. "Please come back to me, Griff."

He kissed her soundly, pulled away, and turned. He was really leaving. Scarlett felt like an elephant was sitting on her chest.

Griff whirled back to her and clasped both of her hands. "Jane." His voice was low and rough. "If I ... don't come back, move on. Be happy. Please."

Scarlett couldn't move or breathe. She wanted to tell him to stop being stupid, call him all kinds of names. How could she move on and be happy without him? He stared at her, begging her to agree. Finally she was able to force out, "No. You come back."

Griff gave her a too-brief and very forced smile and a quick kiss. "Goodbye, Jane."

Then he released her and disappeared into the night. Scarlett stood there, hugging herself, listening to the waves crash. Goodbye, Jane, goodbye. How dare he say goodbye? It should be see you later, see you soon, I love you, anything but goodbye. She wanted to chase after him. She heard doors slamming and a vehicle pulling away out front, and she knew he was gone. Sinking to her knees in the spongy grass, she let herself cry.

CHAPTER TWENTY-THREE

Griff spent weeks tracking down busloads of missing people and working with his men to free them. He realized quickly that it was a Band-Aid fix. This group was too well-organized and effective. He needed to be on the inside. Sutton agreed, and Griff prepared to go deep undercover. The hardest thing to do was send Scarlett the text. He missed her nonstop. Only the knowledge that he was saving hundreds of people kept him from flying home to her each day.

He knew he couldn't get the words out if he heard her lovely voice, so he simply texted, "Going deep undercover. Possibly gone for a few months. Don't plan on any contact. I love you. Be happy."

Her return text was sweet and simple as well. He loved how strong she was and that she didn't demand he call her, or demand he didn't go. She simply said, "I love you more than you know. Please be safe. Please come back to me when you can. Thank you for being the hero."

Griff memorized the words, then informed his parents he'd be out of contact for a while, powered his phone off, handed it to one of his buddies, and asked him to keep it safe.

He'd been growing his hair out since he got to Peru. He got some dirty, ripped clothes, didn't shower for a few days, and prepared himself to pretend to be with the filth of the earth, inside as much as outside. He acted like he was living on the streets of Lima, worked his way into friendship with some of the men he knew worked with the traffickers, and within a few more days he had a job.

The next two months were so horrific that each night he prayed to forget what he'd seen that day. But he saved many, many lives, finding and feeding information on locations, movements, and traffickers' IDs. He had to block out the things he saw, and sometimes even the things he was forced to do, to keep living the lie and saving the highest number of people he could.

He was pretty sure it was the middle of May when he was deep in the slums of Lima. His men hadn't been able to stop this pickup, and he was helping herd refugees into a warehouse where the traffickers would sort the people before shipping them to their most lucrative spot. Two of the men on this crew were as foul as anyone Griff had been around. Many of the girls they'd just brought in were beautiful, and Griff had worried that Joel and Nero would try something. Sure enough, he saw them grabbing two girls each and dragging them away from their families and toward a back room.

Griff followed. This was not happening while he was around. He quietly opened the door. Joel and Nero were busy tying the girls up, but both their heads popped up to glare at Griff.

"Get your own," Joel muttered, standing over a girl who was whimpering.

"No, I want these ones," Griff said. He'd probably ruin his cover, but he couldn't just stand by. He flung himself at Joel, knocking him easily to the floor and banging his head against the rough concrete surface several times. When he was certain the man was knocked out, Griff stood and whirled to take down Nero.

Nero had a gun pointed straight at him. "I never like you, Señor."

Griff smiled and launched himself across the space. He saw Nero pull the trigger, felt the bullet rip through his abdomen, and heard the retort all at the same time. His momentum kept him going forward and he slammed into Nero. The man's body cushioned his fall, but the agony in his abdomen and back was worse than if he'd hit the concrete at the speed he was going.

Nero didn't move, which was satisfying, but Griff quickly realized he couldn't move his legs either. He struggled until he could push the panic button that was sewn into the hem of his pants, praying nobody would hurt these girls before his men came.

Darkness crept around his vision, and he knew he would blessedly pass out soon. Scarlett's face crossed his mind. He loved her, but he realized now why he'd had to say goodbye months ago. He wasn't going to make it back.

CHAPTER TWENTY-FOUR

Scarlett had kept herself very busy during the past few months. She accepted a part in a tragic love story, acting with Christian Ross. He was a great guy and had readily agreed to her request of no love scenes. Even if she hadn't taken the stand to be moral in her movies, she would've made the request since reuniting with Griff. She loved him far too much to pretend to be intimate with another man.

Late one night in May, she was sitting home, grateful that Sutton had set up her current security. She'd never felt so safe, except when Griff was by her side.

A loud rap on her door startled her. She rushed to the cameras and saw Jasmine and Kaleb Quinn standing there. She'd met Kaleb a couple of times at events. Hurrying to open the door, excited to see some of Griff's family, she greeted them with, "Hi! Come in ... Jasmine?"

Jasmine's beautiful face was tear-stained, and she rushed into the entryway and hugged Scarlett tight. Scarlett's stomach dropped. The tough lady would never act like this if something wasn't horribly wrong.

"Griff," Scarlett croaked out.

Kaleb wrapped his arms around both of them and held them tight.

"Griff?" Scarlett could hardly stand to hear the details, but she had to know.

"He's alive," Kaleb said. "He asked us to come."

He was alive. Relief rushed through her, but she knew something bad had happened or they wouldn't be acting like this. "What happened?" Scarlett pulled back from their arms.

Kaleb held on to Jasmine, who still hadn't spoken. "He was shot."

The room spun, and Scarlett sank to the floor. Griff was alive, but he'd been shot. It must have been bad for Jasmine to be mute and looking so horrified.

Jasmine knelt next to her and pulled Scarlett's head into her shoulder. "I'm so sorry, Scarlett. I'm so sorry."

Scarlett's head lifted off Jasmine's shoulder. "You said he's alive," she flung at Kaleb, who was still staring down at the two of them with compassion in his bright blue eyes. Those blue eyes looked far too much like Griff's.

"He is alive." Kaleb cleared his throat and muttered, "They don't dare transport him because ... they think he's paralyzed from the waist down."

Scarlett ripped herself from Jasmine and jumped to her feet. "I have to go to him. Is he still in Peru?" She didn't care about the movie she was working on. She didn't care about anything but Griff.

Jasmine stood and nodded. "Yes, but he wanted us to come explain. He ... doesn't want you there," she said bluntly.

Scarlett backed away, stumbling into an entryway table. The sharp jab to her lower back was nothing compared to the pain in her heart. "Why doesn't he want me?" she asked, the words ripping out of her.

Jasmine shook her head. "Please understand. He loves you so much, but he's a strong, independent man. Probably one of the reasons you love him so much."

Scarlett nodded.

"He needs to work through this and be whole before he comes back to you."

"That is the stupidest thing I've ever heard!" Scarlett yelled. "I want to be there for him and help him heal."

"I know it sounds stupid to you," Jasmine said. "Kaleb feels the exact same way you do, but I understand Griff. He needs physical healing, he needs to come to grips with being paralyzed, but most of all, he needs emotional healing. He can't be the man you need until he can work through his issues. You have to see that." Jasmine's dark eyes were full of begging.

"I don't understand that, at all."

Jasmine nodded. "I know. If you haven't been where Griff and I have been, you couldn't possibly understand it. It took months before I'd let Kaleb love me. It didn't matter how desperately I loved him; I had to heal and know that the Lord could forgive me before I could give myself to Kaleb."

"But why can't he heal with me there, with me helping him?"

Jasmine shook her head. "He has to be strong on his own before he can be strong by your side."

"He's the strongest man I know!"

"Not emotionally, he's not." Jasmine took her hand. "Give him this time, Scarlett." She glanced at her husband. "Kaleb and I both went through agony before I healed enough to be worthy of him."

"Jaz." Kaleb's melodious voice broke into their conversation. "You've always been too good for me."

She gave him a brief smile and corrected, "Before I could *believe* I was worthy of him, worthy of forgiveness." She squeezed Scarlett's hand. "He's got great doctors; the health care in Lima's private sector is very good. Sutton also flew down a spine specialist and neurosurgeon to work with him. Plus, Cannon and his wife, Daisy, volunteered to go stay with him for spiritual support." She stared intently at Scarlett. "Griff's doing everything he can to return to you whole in mind and body. If you truly knew how hardened he's become over the past few years, you'd know him trying to change so he can love you is a miracle in and of itself. Can you trust him and wait?"

Scarlett shook her head and blinked quickly. "I don't know," she admitted.

"Do it for him," Jasmine requested.

"You know I'd do anything for him."

"Good." Jasmine's voice lowered. "Because the next few weeks are going to be the worst of your life."

Scarlett thought that was the most accurate thing Jasmine had said tonight.

Griff had known pain in so many forms that by now he simply accepted it as part of his life. The pain he went through in the weeks after his accident was horrific. The therapy to heal his back and bring life back into his legs hurt, which the doctors kept reassuring him was a "wonderful thing." The pain of healing internally, without reaching for his phone and calling Scarlett, was worse.

Cannon, a former Navy SEAL and their volunteer chaplain, arrived the day after he was shot. Griff scoffed when Cannon explained he and his wife, Daisy, had come to heal him inside, though deep down Griff knew it was what he needed.

The person he really wanted at his side was Scarlett. He wanted to believe he was worthy of her and could have a great life with her, but how did he simply bury the agony of always remembering the people he had hurt, the lives he had taken?

Being shot and thinking he was dying had changed him, but he was still a warrior inside and wanted more than anything to return to the battle. There were too many people who needed protecting for him to simply give it up. Yet if he didn't put that life behind him, how could he be with Scarlett? How could he ask her to keep loving him if he wasn't whole in mind and body and if he kept killing or ended up dead?

He grew very close to Cannon and Daisy. Griff would have rejected anyone else, but Cannon had been there—killed people, was held captive, tortured, and had not only found his peace, but helped a few of Sutton's other guys to do so. As Griff's back healed and he pushed himself to regain movement and strength in his legs, Cannon worked with him to turn his heart to God and let him heal his insides, understand that he could be a warrior and a God-fearing man.

At first he resisted, making it harder than the therapy for his lower body, but slowly he started listening, internalizing, and trusting. He felt more hope for his future than he ever had. He loved God and he loved Scarlett. She was his choice and his dream, yet still he hadn't picked up the phone to call her. He determined he wanted to walk in her door and show her he was whole. He prayed that miracle would happen soon, but he was learning that the Lord's timetable was much different from his. Patience was the roughest part of his healing process. Patience had never been his strength.

CHAPTER TWENTY-FIVE

Griff flew into a small airport in San Diego at eight a.m. Someone told him it was June twentieth. He'd lost almost a month to therapy. Cannon and Daisy had stayed by his side through all of it, and they now exited the plane with him. He was walking, but slowly. Physically, he was a broken shell of himself. Emotionally, he'd never been stronger. All that mattered to him now was finding Scarlett and begging her to forgive and love him.

He gave his close friends both a long hug. "Thank you" was so insufficient, but he didn't know what else to say, so in true Griff fashion, he stayed silent. They walked away happily, hand in hand.

Griff shuffled to the Escalade where Sutton was waiting. Sutton shook his hand and clasped his shoulder. "I'm proud of you, son."

"Sir." He nodded his gratitude.

"Where to?"

"Scarlett Lily's house."

Sutton smiled. "I actually have intel that she's about to go live on the daytime talk show, Jessie. She's doing the segment after your little brother, Mack, and his fiancé, Sariah Udy."

Griff processed this. "Can you get me in the audience, sir?"

"I'll make some phone calls on the way." Sutton swung open his door.

Griff climbed inside. Sitting was the most uncomfortable position for him, but he didn't care. He was going to see Scarlett soon. He prayed she wouldn't hate him for waiting so long. He'd needed this time to heal, to strengthen himself from the inside out, and to know he was worthy of Scarlett. He smiled to himself. No one was worthy of his Jane, but he would do all he could to care for her like she should be cared for.

Sutton climbed in and smiled at him. "It's great to have you back."

"I don't know that I'll ever be back, sir." His injury was going to take a lot of time to heal, and even with all the therapy he'd been through, he still didn't trust himself not to rush at the gun rather than duck like any sane person would do. If Scarlett would marry him, he would shift his focus. He would find a way to right wrongs without being in the middle of the battle.

"I've been thinking about you a lot, Griff. I have so many men and women working for me, all with different skill sets. You and

River are the best at combat of anyone I know, and with Ally expecting ..."

"Congrats. You'll be a grandpa."

Sutton grinned. "Liz and I are thrilled." He went on. "River wants to step out of combat, and I expect your Scarlett Lily might like you doing the same."

Griff's heart thumped faster. *If* Scarlett forgave him for ditching her and going dark these past few months. He worried that she'd be angry and not want him anymore. "She'd never ask it of me, but I think it might be the right path."

"Would you consider training for me?"

Griff nodded. "I would, sir."

"Cheers." Sutton put the vehicle into gear and pushed the button to make a call. Griff listened as Sutton was quickly patched through to the executive of the television studio. Of course he found the top man. Sutton could move mountains with his connections.

Griff shifted, trying to get comfortable in the seat. He was almost to Scarlett. Relying on the faith of his youth, the faith he'd rediscovered the past month, he bowed his head and prayed she still loved him.

Scarlett waited for her part on Jessie's show. She'd talked with Mack Quinn and Sariah Udy briefly before they walked hand in hand onto the stage. They were such a beautiful couple, and as she watched their sweet love from offstage, she couldn't help but ache for Griff. Not that the ache was new, but it seemed stronger watching this man, who looked like a larger, younger version of Griff, holding his fiancée's hand and beaming at her.

Looking over the audience from next to the stage, Scarlett saw many of the Quinn family were there supporting the couple. If only she'd blink and Griff would be there. Was he still in Peru? Was he in a wheelchair, or had he healed? She'd gone to Kaleb and Jasmine, to Sutton, begging for information about him, especially the address to go find him. They all repeatedly told her he was progressing well and to just give him time. Her heart kept breaking over and over again.

"It's time," the assistant next to her whispered.

Scarlett nodded, put her actor shutter on, and strode onto the stage. She waved to the audience, smiling as they clapped ecstatically for her.

A man was slowly walking down the aisle—a well-built man in a button-down shirt and slacks with short dark blond hair and the most handsome face she'd ever seen. Griff! Scarlett paused a few feet from Jessie and gaped at him. He met her gaze and smiled. His smile was so brilliant, so perfect, and his eyes were warm.

He was here! Happiness burst from her, but immediately doubts crept in. If he was in America, why hadn't he come directly to her? He wasn't in a wheelchair, but he was obviously in pain judging by the way he moved.

"Come sit." Jessie had a hold of her hand and was tugging her toward the side-by-side chairs.

Scarlett snapped back to reality of being on live national television. The things she needed to hear from Griff would have to wait … unless he stormed the stage and took her in his arms. She was still living in her dream world. Griff was an undercover op specialist. He couldn't just walk onto stage and proclaim he loved her, no matter how much she wanted him to.

She tried to focus on the host and what she was saying, but inside she couldn't stop praying that Griff would come for her after the show. He'd claimed in Island Park that he didn't want to hurt her anymore. If that was true, she had no clue how he could be here and not hold her close. Somehow she had to get through this show; then she was tracking him down.

CHAPTER TWENTY-SIX

Griff was slowly making his way down the aisle toward where his family sat when Scarlett strode out onto the stage. She was absolutely gorgeous—her long, blonde hair streaming behind her, her beautiful face grinning at the audience, her perfect form displayed in a tailored floral blouse and a straight blue skirt. She was still blonde. Was that for him?

She saw him and paused in the middle of the stage. Their gazes connected and he grinned at her, praying she would know that he was here for her now, how much he loved her, how sorry he was that he'd hurt her again. He wanted to run onto the stage and sweep her into his arms. Unfortunately, he wouldn't be running for a long, long time, and this probably wasn't the right moment to declare his undying love for her.

The host grasped her elbow and escorted her to the chairs, ending their moment. Griff sank into a seat next to Navy. She gave him a brief hug. "Welcome home, bro," she whispered.

"Good to be here," he grunted back. He waved to the rest of his family, all watching him. His mama looked ready to jump up and fling herself at him, but he'd held himself aloof from everyone for so long that she just gave him a big smile and blew him a kiss, tears streaming down her face. He promised himself that after he found Scarlett, he would hold his mama and tell her how much he loved her, tell her how sorry he was for causing her anguish for so many years.

He turned and focused on the stage as Jessie gushed over Scarlett.

"You've stayed blonde," Jessie was saying.

"Yes."

"A lot of your fans aren't happy about it."

Scarlett laughed. He loved her laugh. "You should talk to my agent and producer if you want to see not happy."

So nobody wanted her blonde but him. Was it for him? Griff's mind went, as it often did, to that brief time they'd been together in Island Park. Those memories had motivated and strengthened him for the past three months. It was torture to have her right in front of him and not be able to go scoop her up and hold her close, tell her how much he loved her. How would she react if he did?

Jessie was asking about her new movie, and he focused in on Scarlett's answer. "When I saw this script, it was like it was written for me."

"Really?" The talk show host leaned closer to her, eager for this insight into Scarlett Lily's thoughts. Griff found himself leaning too. He ached for her.

"I haven't done a romance for a long time, but I fell in love for the second time a few months ago." She smiled, and Griff could've sworn she was smiling only for him.

She still loved him. It was all he could do to not punch a fist into the air, or better yet, go to her.

"When you love deeply, it's easier to act the part." She gave a soft laugh.

Griff's heart thundered in his chest. She loved *him* deeply.

"But doesn't the love of her life leave her for the war ... and die?"

Scarlett nodded. "'Death cannot stop true love.'"

She'd told him that not even death could separate them. It was true. Right now, he wanted to live for her. He'd almost died in Peru. Was it finally their time to love?

Jessie laughed. "Quoting *Princess Bride*? I love it." She arched an eyebrow. "Are the rumors true that you wouldn't do a love scene with Christian Ross? How could you resist being close to that beautiful man?"

Griff's heart was beating so hard, he was starting to feel lightheaded. Navy took his hand and held it. His older sister was too protective of all of the brothers, but even she had been forced to distance herself from Griff over the years.

Instead of pulling his hand free, Griff squeezed her hand back, grateful for the support. Navy had tried to grill him months ago about Scarlett, and of course he'd brushed her off. Yet she was an intuitive sister. It had to be obvious to anyone within a hundred yards how smitten he was with Scarlett.

"The decision was mutual," Scarlett said. "You know he's happily married."

"But you instigated the agreement?"

Scarlett nodded. "I've always stayed away from romance scripts for this very reason. I believe intimacy is sacred and shouldn't be shown onscreen or even acted out with anyone other than one's husband or wife."

"That's a bold statement—and one that might offend your viewers."

Scarlett shrugged. "It's not about being popular. It's about being true to myself and my beliefs—and the man I love."

Griff's heart seemed to explode within his chest. *True to the man I love*. This interview had better be over quick, or he'd have no choice but to interrupt it, pushing his way onto the stage and holding Scarlett. He glanced around for security, certain he could get past them even with his injury.

"Oh my! So when are you going to reveal this love? There are no pictures of you with anyone."

Scarlett gave a very practiced smile, but then her eyes flitted to him and her face softened, love for him shining in her eyes. "That's up to him. I'm respecting his choices."

That was it. Griff used the seat in front of him to lumber to his feet.

"Go get her, bro," Navy encouraged him.

Griff gave her a thumbs-up, but he was focused on Scarlett. The interview lady was talking, but Scarlett didn't answer her; her eyes were fixed on Griff as he walked down the aisle as quickly as his beat-up body would allow. Most of his undercover ops would be over when he declared himself the love of Scarlett Lily's life. All that mattered to him was his Jane. Did she truly still want him? She was the most beautiful and amazing woman he knew.

He didn't see security storming toward him, and even the prattling show host had stopped talking. The audience hushed as well, sensing something out of the ordinary had happened.

The Griff of a month ago would've been humiliated for the world to see how slow he moved, how humble he was for Scarlett. Now all Griff wanted was Scarlett, and he couldn't wait a second more to tell her he was sorry, pull her into his arms, and never let her go.

Griff slowly made his way toward the stage, so handsome and strong despite the agonizing way he moved. Their gazes locked, and his face softened. The studio was quiet as all eyes were focused on the man she had been praying would return for her.

He was almost to the steps when she heard his quiet whisper. "Jane."

Scarlett gave a little whimper and rushed down the stairs and into the aisle. He opened his arms. As she threw herself against his chest, he grunted and stuttered, but he held steady.

Scarlett pulled back quickly. "Oh no, did I hurt you?"

"Yeah." Griff nodded seriously, but his eyes twinkled. "You're hurting me by not kissing me right now."

She gave a strangled laugh, and he wrapped her up tight. He bowed his head to kiss her, capturing her mouth with a passion and love that was all Griff. No one could ever replace him, and he was finally holding her. She loved every part of him.

The audience was cheering raucously around them, but she couldn't have cared less. She wasn't playing for any audience. All that mattered to her was Griff.

He pulled back, and his brilliantly blue eyes caressed her as surely as his mouth had. "I'm so sorry, Jane. So sorry I didn't let you come to me. So sorry I've hurt you. I've prayed so hard that you'd forgive me, wished you were with me to tell me how stupid I've been." He gave a lopsided grin. "But I had to heal ... everywhere. I had to turn myself to God to be worthy of you."

"Jasmine tried to explain," she told him. "I wanted to be there with you, for you, but all that matters is that you're healed and you're here now." She'd forgive him every time, but she didn't want him to leave her side again.

Jessie was suddenly next to them. "Are we going to get an introduction to the man in your life?"

Scarlett glanced around. Cameras and people and the life she knew so well. She smiled and shook her head. "No. I'm keeping him all to myself."

Griff laughed, and to her surprise, he released his right hand from around her back and offered it to Jessie. "Griff Quinn. It's a pleasure."

"Quinn? As in the brother to Mack, Ryder, Colt, Navy, and Kaleb?" Her voice pitched up in surprise at this happy tidbit that she was able to share with the world. The only not-so-famous Quinn brother, the warrior, and Scarlett Lily. This was already going viral, guaranteed.

"Yes, ma'am." He wrapped his arm around Scarlett's waist again. "If you'll excuse us, please. I need some time alone with my girl."

"Well, don't let us keep you."

"I won't." Griff gifted her with his irresistible grin.

Jessie moaned, "Oh, have mercy."

He tightened his grip on Scarlett's waist, and she cuddled in close to him. Their progress was agonizingly slow, but she didn't care what anyone watching thought. Griff had come for her. He'd strode onto a national television show and introduced himself for her. She knew it hadn't been easy to show the world he was injured and to show the world his face, but he did it for her.

The crowd cheered them on, and a security person directed them out a side door and into a hallway where they could finally be alone.

Griff smiled down at her, leaning down and capturing her mouth with his. The kiss was everything she'd always dreamed of. Scarlett wrapped her arms around his strong shoulders and held on.

When they pulled apart, she wanted to just kiss him again, but she had to know. "Why didn't you come for me as soon as you got home?"

"I flew in an hour ago. I was headed straight for your house, but Sutton, of course, had the intel you were here. He got me into the show."

"Sometimes I like Sutton." Griff *had* come for her after all.

He chuckled. "When don't you like him?"

"When he takes you away from me."

Griff nodded and brushed the hair from her face. "Have I told you I love you as a blonde?"

"You're dodging the issue."

"So the cease-fire is over?"

"No, the cease-fire can last fifty years if we need. But it would be fabulous to know that I can hold you for longer than five minutes."

He smiled. "Sutton's asked me to train his people in the art of combat. I'm going to help with the battle, but not be in the middle of it for now."

She squealed and kissed him soundly. Griff pulled her toward the wall and leaned against it.

"Are you really okay?" she asked.

"I've never been better." His voice lowered and he murmured, "I can't even tell you how much I've missed you. I love you, Jane."

She gazed up at his handsome face, bursting with love for him. "Only you get the privilege of calling me Jane."

"Jane, Scarlett." He tenderly cupped her cheek with his palm, brushing his lips over hers and making her quiver from head to toe. "What do you want me to call you, love?"

Scarlett smiled. "That."

"What?"

"Love."

His grin grew, and he pulled her close. "Love it is."

Don't miss the rest of the Quinn family series:

Quinn Romance Adventures
Devoted & Deserted
Conflicted & Famous
Gentle & Broken
Rugged & At-Risk
Too-Perfect & Stranded
Rejected & Hidden

EXCERPT: GENTLE & BROKEN

Mack Quinn, offensive lineman for the Georgia Patriots, followed the crowd of his teammates as they surged toward Hyde Metcalf, their wide receiver, to celebrate the winning touchdown pass. A win against Dallas on Christmas Day was great vindication after Dallas had beaten the Patriots out of their spot in the Super Bowl last year. Teammates slapped Hyde on the shoulder and someone hoisted their quarterback, Rigby "the Rocket" Breeland, into the air, but Hyde Metcalf dodged anyone trying to slow him down.

Staying close to his fellow linemen, Mack tried to keep up with Hyde, and blend in with the crowd. Not an easy feat when you were six-eight and over three hundred pounds. Luckily, Mack could move fast, even if his siblings and teammates teased him that he was built like a Mack truck.

He approached the sidelines and watched as Hyde launched himself over the barrier and into the waiting arms of his fiancée,

Lily Udy. Mack's gaze didn't linger on the couple kissing, he searched for the young woman who accompanied Hyde's mom and fiancée to every game. He stopped in his tracks and let out an audible sigh. Sariah Udy.

Somebody ran into him from behind, but he couldn't do more than mutter, "It's okay," to their apology. The woman of his dreams was less than ten feet away from him ... and she had absolutely no clue that he existed. Sariah was cheering, along with her family, as Hyde and Lily kissed and then Hyde started hugging everybody.

He waited directly below Sariah, praying she'd glance his way, he started second-guessing himself. Just because he'd fallen hopelessly for her didn't mean she even knew who he was. Maybe all these times he thought she'd been tangling glances with him, she'd truly just been watching the game, or worse, she'd been staring at Tate Campbell or somebody like that who could flirt with a woman like her without their tongue swelling in their mouth.

Sariah finished helping Hyde's mom. The family was still focused on Hyde and Sariah's little brother, Josh, as he exclaimed over the game. Sariah's gaze traveled around the team slowly. Was she searching for him? Mack wanted to yell, "I'm here! Look down." But he didn't. He was the biggest chicken he knew.

Sariah finally seemed to sense him staring at her and her eyes met his. Mack tried to sputter out a hello, but he couldn't have said anything to save even his mama's life.

A slow grin curved Sariah's full lips and her deep brown eyes sparkled at him. She pulled her hair forward on the right side, twisting it in front of her neck. Mack was panting for air worse than when they made him run sprints at practice. He savored every second of the connection, knowing it couldn't last. He'd never gotten this close to her, but he'd watched her after every home game of the season. She'd head up the stairs with her sister and Hyde's mom soon and he'd be left watching her go, like always.

Instead of turning away she stepped right up to the railing, leaned over, and reached her hand down, still giving him that beautiful and inviting smile. Mack's heart leapt. He felt like a loyal knight who might get the opportunity to touch the beautiful princess' hand after winning the tournament.

Usually, Mack was light and fast on his feet, even with his large size. Right now, he lumbered forward, his size fourteen feet felt like blocks of cement, and all he wanted was to get close to her faster.

Finally, he reached the wall and luckily, he was tall enough he didn't have to reach up very far to wrap his hand around her delicate fingers. A zing of awareness and warmth shot through him. His brain tried to keep up with his heart but his heart was singing too loud, *Sariah Udy is holding my hand!*

She smiled down at him. The smile was sweet and welcoming and all the oxygen rushed out of Mack's body. He could face down the most vicious defenders on the field, but he had no clue how to react to holding Sariah's hand and having her smile at him like that.

The roaring crowd around them disappeared as they focused on each other. Mack knew right at that moment—he was in serious like and he had to do something about it. He'd dated different girls throughout high school, college, and the past couple of years women had chased him relentlessly, but he'd never felt a connection like this. This had to be the right woman for him.

"Hi," she said softly.

"Hi," Mack dumbly repeated. He squeezed her hand, he hoped gently, and searched his muddled brain for something poetic to say. His brother, Kaleb, was a professional country singer and had all manner of beautiful things to say or sing. His brother, Colt, was a professional woman-magnet and had trained Mack relentlessly on how to give a woman a smoldering look or say the right phrase to draw her in.

Mack prayed for inspiration and finally muttered, "Hi, pretty girl."

His face flamed red. What had he just said? He probably sounded like a creeper or something. That line had worked on his older brothers' girlfriends when Mack was eight and cute. Now he was twenty-five and hopefully there was nothing cute about him.

Sariah let out a soft chuckle and then tugged her hand free, waved quickly to him, and hurried to her family. Mack watched them all walk away. Her dad gave him a backwards, concerned glance, but Sariah didn't turn around or acknowledge him again.

Mack felt like he'd been slugged in the abdomen by his brother, Griff, the ex-navy SEAL who could take down any man. His big chance and he'd messed it all up. *Hi, pretty girl?* Sheesh, he was an idiot.

Find *Gentle & Broken* on Amazon.

EXCERPT - TOO-PERFECT & STRANDED

Navy took a break from freestyle and changed to breaststroke. She loved the warm water gliding past her body and decided she would swim all the way around the small island. If she got lucky, she'd see Holden sailing in once she made it around to the south.

Water rhythmically splashed behind her and Navy turned to look. A man was swimming toward her with quick, powerful strokes. Her first reaction was panic, thinking Ryan was chasing her. She didn't think the buff trainer would try to attack her, but she had never let herself be alone with him, just in case. Out here at the rear of the island, she could hardly even see the house. There would be no help coming if it was Ryan or another man who might hurt her.

Looking closer, she realized the man's coloring was much darker than Ryan's. She'd assumed it was only the *Muscle Up* crew on the island this week but maybe there was a caretaker? She squinted, wondering if it might be Holden, but she couldn't be sure. Whoever it was they must be some swimmer to be moving that fast.

She wasn't willing to risk being alone with an unknown man so she fell back into swimming and pushed herself around the back of the island, hoping she could make it to the bay where Holden's yacht would pull in soon and everyone would be busy unloading supplies. Her brother, Griff, a former Navy SEAL had taught her how to protect herself, but he'd been adamant that the best protection was to never be in a situation where a man could take advantage of her. She was tough, but she was small, and men were naturally stronger.

"Navy!"

She surfaced at sound of the familiar voice calling her name. The man had gained on her quickly and now was treading water a short distance away and grinning at her. The air rushed out of her body and Navy was grateful for the saltiness of the water making it easier to stay afloat. Holden Jennings was here and apparently chasing her around the island in the water. It might not mean anything to him, but it made her heart beat faster. He probably wanted to have a business meeting. In the gorgeous Caribbean ocean. In swimsuits. This water was really warm. She was sweating and splashed some water on her cheeks.

"Hey," she called back.

Holden did the breaststroke toward her, giving her the advantage of staring at his lovely shoulders and arms as he swam and his even lovelier face and smile as he approached. "Lovely" was a silly word to describe such a tough and perfectly handsome man, but she liked to use it. She could convince herself that "lovely" was mocking her perfect boss. He was *too* perfect. That was his fault. His manners were impeccable; he was wealthy, accomplished, hard-working, kind, funny. ... Too perfect. She definitely didn't want a man who was too perfect. How boring would that be? Boring or not, she couldn't resist staring and sighing softly as he got closer.

"How are you?" he asked as he finally reached her. She suddenly felt stupid. She'd made him swim the entire distance toward her as she treaded water and stared unabashedly at him.

"Fabulous. You?" Navy slowly milled her legs and arms in the water.

"Better now," he said, his grin growing. "Isn't she beautiful?"

"The island?"

But he wasn't looking at the island. He was staring straight at her. Holden gave a short laugh and splashed some water at her. "Yes, the island."

Navy dragged her arm through the water and gave him a mouthful. "Not as beautiful as that," Navy yelled, surprising herself with her impetuous response. She'd longed to be impetuous with this man and given the slightest opportunity, impetuous came very naturally.

Holden's eyes widened and then narrowed mischievously. Navy had seen that look on one of her brother's faces far too often. She dodged away, but Holden caught hold of her arm and dragged her under the water.

Navy came up spluttering. Holden chuckled. "Teach you to throw water at me."

"Oh, I'll teach you." Navy threw caution to the wind as she reacted exactly the way she'd always wanted to with Holden and launched herself at him, wrapped her arms around his head and tried to dunk him. He was too strong for her to push under.

Holden responded by wrapping his arms tight around her waist, pulling her against his firm chest and taking them both under water. They both came up spluttering and laughing, but then Navy realized she was clinging to the beautiful Holden Jennings as he held them both up. Fire raced through her for two reasons—how fabulous his strong body felt against hers and embarrassment that she was acting completely unprofessional. She and Holden had known each other a long time and they were good friends and comfortable with each other, but they'd never grabbed each other or messed around, especially not while wearing swimsuits. No matter that she'd often daydreamed about such moments, she shouldn't be acting on those silly fantasies.

The moment seemed to slow down as Holden released her and they stared at each other, both treading water, still far too close together for Navy's susceptible heart. She wondered if she should apologize for acting immature and too familiar with him, but he'd been part of it too. Instead she slowly edged away from him and said, "Do I need to get ready for the first shoot?"

He shook his head. "I didn't come after you for that."

"Oh, really?" She arched her eyebrows and dared him to admit why he came after her.

He stared at her for a few beats, his deep brown eyes warm and far too attractive with those long lashes framing them and his dark eyebrows completing the look. His short facial hair outlined his mouth. Oh, how she loved just the right amount of beard on a man. She needed to think of something wrong with him, and quick. His mouth! That was it. She'd finally found his fault. His mouth was too … perfect. Dang it, that was the only word for it. His lips were just thick enough to keep it interesting and the top lip had the most intriguing bow to it. How she'd dreamed of kissing his top lip, then his bottom lip, then …

"Navy?"

"What? What just happened?" She blinked and swam past him toward the shore.

"Are you okay?" He was right by her side.

"No. I'm … dizzy."

Holden immediately spun her onto her back in the water, secured his arm over her chest, and started tugging her toward the beach. All kinds of wanton feelings rushed over her at his touch.

"What are you doing?" she sputtered.

"You're okay." His voice was soothing. "I was a lifeguard. We're almost to the beach."

Of course he was a lifeguard. He'd probably starred in Baywatch. She felt ridiculous as he dragged her through the water. The strength in the arm that was holding her was impressive. She wanted to wrap her hand around his bicep and forearm, but what she really needed was some distance or she was going to throw caution to the tropical breeze, act completely unprofessional, and no one could hold her responsible for it.

Find *Too-Perfect & Stranded* on Amazon.

ALSO BY CAMI CHECKETTS

Quinn Romance Adventures

Devoted & Deserted

Conflicted & Famous

Gentle & Broken

Rugged & At-Risk

Too-Perfect & Stranded

Rejected & Hidden

Billionaire Protection Romances

Matchmaking the Singer and the Warrior

Matchmaking the Fitness Trainer and the Commander

Matchmaking the Entertainer and the Firefighter

Summit Valley Christmas Romance

His Perfect Match for Christmas

His Ski Resort Overrun for Christmas

His Cabin Invaded for Christmas

His Unexpected Wedding for Christmas

Delta Family Romances

Deceived

Abandoned

Committed

Betrayed

Devoted

Compromised

Endangered

Accepted

Returned

Devastated

Famous Friends Romances

Loving the Firefighter

Loving the Athlete

Loving the Rancher

Loving the Coach

Loving the Contractor

Loving the Sheriff

Loving the Entertainer

The Hidden Kingdom Romances

Royal Secrets

Royal Security

Royal Doctor

Royal Mistake

Royal Courage

Royal Pilot

Royal Imposter

Royal Baby

Royal Battle

Royal Fake Fiancé

Secret Valley Romance

Sister Pact

Marriage Pact

Christmas Pact

Survive the Romance

Romancing the Treasure

Romancing the Escape

Romancing the Boat

Romancing the Mountain

Romancing the Castle

Romancing the Extreme Adventure

Romancing the Island

Romancing the River

Romancing the Spartan Race

Mystical Lake Resort Romance

Only Her Undercover Spy

Only Her Cowboy

Only Her Best Friend

Only Her Blue-Collar Billionaire

Only Her Injured Stuntman

Only Her Amnesiac Fake Fiancé

Only Her Hockey Legend

Only Her Smokejumper Firefighter

Only Her Christmas Miracle

Jewel Family Romance

Do Marry Your Billionaire Boss

Do Trust Your Special Ops Bodyguard

Do Date Your Handsome Rival

Do Rely on Your Protector

Do Kiss the Superstar

Do Tease the Charming Billionaire

Do Claim the Tempting Athlete

Do Depend on Your Keeper

Strong Family Romance

Don't Date Your Brother's Best Friend

Her Loyal Protector

Don't Fall for a Fugitive

Her Hockey Superstar Fake Fiance

Don't Ditch a Detective

Don't Miss the Moment

Don't Love an Army Ranger

Don't Chase a Player

Don't Abandon the Superstar

Steele Family Romance

Her Dream Date Boss

The Stranded Patriot

The Committed Warrior

Extreme Devotion

Running Romcom

Running for Love

Taken from Love

Saved by Love

Cami's Collections

Hidden Kingdom Romance Collection

Survive the Romance Collection

Mystical Lake Resort Romance Collection

Billionaire Boss Romance Collection

Jewel Family Collection

The Romance Escape Collection

Cami's Firefighter Collection

Strong Family Romance Collection

Steele Family Collection

Hawk Brothers Collection

Quinn Family Collection

Cami's Georgia Patriots Collection

Cami's Military Collection

Billionaire Beach Romance Collection

Billionaire Bride Pact Collection

Echo Ridge Romance Collection

Texas Titans Romance Collection

Snow Valley Collection

Christmas Romance Collection

Holiday Romance Collection

Extreme Sports Romance Collection

Georgia Patriots Romance

The Loyal Patriot

The Gentle Patriot

The Stranded Patriot

The Pursued Patriot

Jepson Brothers Romance

How to Design Love

How to Switch a Groom

How to Lose a Fiance

Billionaire Boss Romance

Her Dream Date Boss

Her Prince Charming Boss

Hawk Brothers Romance

The Determined Groom

The Stealth Warrior

Her Billionaire Boss Fake Fiance

Risking it All

Navy Seal Romance

The Protective Warrior

The Captivating Warrior

The Stealth Warrior

The Tough Warrior

Texas Titan Romance

The Fearless Groom

The Trustworthy Groom

The Beastly Groom

The Irresistible Groom

The Determined Groom

The Devoted Groom

Billionaire Beach Romance

Caribbean Rescue

Cozumel Escape

Cancun Getaway

Trusting the Billionaire

How to Kiss a Billionaire

Onboard for Love

Shadows in the Curtain

Billionaire Bride Pact Romance

The Resilient One

The Feisty One

The Independent One

The Protective One

The Faithful One

The Daring One

Park City Firefighter Romance

Rescued by Love

Reluctant Rescue

Stone Cold Sparks

Snowed-In for Christmas

Echo Ridge Romance

Christmas Makeover

Last of the Gentlemen

My Best Man's Wedding

Change of Plans

Counterfeit Date

Snow Valley

Full Court Devotion: Christmas in Snow Valley

A Touch of Love: Summer in Snow Valley

Running from the Cowboy: Spring in Snow Valley

Light in Your Eyes: Winter in Snow Valley

Romancing the Singer: Return to Snow Valley

Fighting for Love: Return to Snow Valley

Other Books by Cami

Seeking Mr. Debonair: Jane Austen Pact

Seeking Mr. Dependable: Jane Austen Pact

Saving Sycamore Bay

Oh, Come On, Be Faithful

Protect This

Blog This

Redeem This

The Broken Path

Dead Running

Dying to Run

Fourth of July

Love & Loss

Love & Lies

ABOUT THE AUTHOR

Cami is a part-time author, part-time exercise consultant, part-time housekeeper, full-time wife, and overtime mother of four adorable boys. Sleep and relaxation are fond memories. She's never been happier.

Join Cami's VIP list to find out about special deals, giveaways and new releases and receive a free copy of *Rescued by Love: Park City Firefighter Romance* by clicking here.

cami@camichecketts.com
www.camichecketts.com

1ST CHAPTER - MATCHMAKING THE SINGER AND THE WARRIOR

Gray Denizen, Smokey G to most of the world, sat in the steaming hot tub on the deck of his Wengen rental home overlooking the picturesque, snow-covered Lauterbrunnen Valley in the Swiss Alps. The sun had set while he marinated in the water, and the valley of seventy waterfalls, the real home of the Hobbit, was now just some twinkling lights far below. He loved it here. He wanted to come back in the summer and hike, bike, and soar down the mountain slopes with a parasail, see it green and flowering instead of covered with mounds of snow. It was insanely beautiful with its blanket of white. He could only imagine the mystical beauty of this area when it was lush and green.

The snow skiing for Christmas had been insane, but all his friends had gone back to "real life." They loved to tease him that his life was a vacation, but Gray's life was his work. He loved composing songs and recording them. He didn't love the endless travel, performing in front of huge and raucous crowds, or all the details involved with social media, mainstream media, and being concerned that any word he spoke might be misconstrued.

He'd finished his European tour right before Christmas and sent his staff and assistant, Janie, home for the holidays. Instead of going to his house on the Fort Lauderdale intercoastal, he'd begged some friends to come here. Janie had found this unreal mountainside village, only accessible by train or helicopter. He'd had to opt for the helicopter simply to keep fans from seeing him and letting it slip where he was. Apparently, he was in danger. He was always in danger, had been since childhood, so it didn't bother him much.

The few single friends who he trusted not to post on social media or brag about spending Christmas with him, had met him here. They'd skied the famed Wengen, Grindelwald, and Jungfrau resorts. Incredible. And he'd been able to stay incognito with helmet, goggles, and a face shield on. No Russian mafia busting through the front door to ruin the holidays.

But now he was semi-alone. He was used to his assistant Janie, his cook Liam, his personal trainer Joseph, his two incredible housekeepers Quincy and Nellie, plus millions of fans looking for any opportunity to talk to, stare at, or touch him. It was odd to have true peace and quiet. His security guys were still here, of course, led and trained by his stepdad, Russ.

The four tough men claimed they had to stay with him. There'd been some backlash about him helping a beautiful woman escape her Russian mafia-affiliated boyfriend, so now his security team refused to leave his side. Apparently, even if you were a famous billionaire singer, you didn't mess with the Russian mafia. What was the good of being famous and wealthy if you couldn't right some wrongs in the world?

He swirled the hot water between his fingers. He should get out, fix himself something to eat, read, and go to bed. In a few days, he'd fly to Grand Cayman and his staff would meet him there. They'd have two weeks to relax on the beach, which usually meant beach runs, lifting weights, and long hours working on new song lyrics. He'd start a short five-stop tour of the Caribbean Islands after that. He'd thought he wanted these few days after Christmas to decompress, but peace and quiet alone wasn't all it was cracked up to be.

He liked and appreciated all of his security guards, but with twelve-hour shifts either monitoring the cameras they'd set up in the basement or doing their rounds inside and outside the house, they only had twelve hours off to sleep, exercise, run to get groceries or supplies, or have a bit of free time. He tried not to bug them during their moments off, unless they offered to spar or lift with him.

Great guys, most especially his stepdad, Captain Russell Brown. Gray loved and respected Russ above anyone in this world. He knew the retired Marine felt the same, but he wasn't exactly a profuse or friendly person. Tim, Kaden, and Cameron were each twenty years younger than Russ, give or take a few years. They were all willing to go pick up dinner, help keep things clean without the housekeepers here, have a conversation with him, or work out with him, but none of them were big on brainstorming song lyrics or discussing the latest clean romance novel he was reading. He smiled to himself. Not that he'd admit he read clean romance.

A thud came from around the side of the house. Gray straightened, staring that direction, but with the low lights glowing through the three-story windows behind him, he couldn't see anything. A dart of apprehension made the hot tub feel even hotter. Had the Russian mafia somehow found out where he was? The house had been rented in an umbrella company's name that wasn't affiliated with his name at all, and he hadn't so much as gone to dinner or anywhere besides skiing, where his face had been completely covered.

He'd waved to Tim a few minutes ago as he'd walked by the side of the massive patio through one of the trails he and the guys had dug into the deep snow. The backside of the patio dropped off into nothingness, so at least there was one angle that couldn't be approached without a lot of tactical gear.

Scrambling out of the hot tub, Gray's bare feet hit the cold patio and steam rose from his body. His body temperature was high enough from his soak and the quickening of his pulse that he welcomed the piercing cold air.

Not bothering with the stack of towels, he hurried to the edge of the patio where Tim should be monitoring, and tried to peer into the darkness. If there was trouble, more of his men would come running, but Gray knew his way around a fight. He'd been raised in East L.A., and he'd learned young how to keep him and his mom safe from thugs—and his own father.

"Tim?" he questioned.

A small person sprang out of the darkness and knocked him flat on his back. Gray bucked his body and rolled, holding on to the person's arms and pinning his assailant underneath his much larger frame.

His attacker was a ... woman. His eyes widened. An exquisitely beautiful woman. He could only stare in shock as she smiled sweetly up at him, her blue eyes lit with mischief and her smooth skin crinkling at the edges of her lips and her eyes. Her gorgeous smile conveyed she was ecstatic he was pinning her down.

He felt a rush of desire fill him that was completely out of line for the situation. This woman had attacked him. He should be afraid, or at least annoyed. Was she an ultra-fan, affiliated with someone who was targeting him, or a completely different kind of danger? Sparks swirled between them and her small frame underneath him felt really, really nice. He listened for other sounds, but the night was still. Was she alone? Where were his men? Even if she'd bested Tim, which was highly unlikely, someone would've seen this woman knocking Gray down on the cameras. They should be bursting out the patio door with guns drawn.

"Well, hello, handsome." She was slightly out of breath, probably because he was twice her size and pinning her down, but he liked the sound of her voice and the breathlessness of it. "I liked the reversal. Don't tell anyone I let you get away with that. I have a reputation of ruthlessness to uphold."

He almost laughed at her smart-aleck response, but he realized immediately ... This woman wasn't a fan or dangerous to him. He knew her, and he really shouldn't be feeling sparks of desire, or be pinning down, this famous and very happily married woman. Why was Scarlett Lily sneaking onto his back patio and knocking him down when she should be in California with her husband and son? It was out of character for her to flirt with or tease anyone besides her husband.

"Scarlett?" he questioned, easing off her, standing, and offering a hand up. She took his hand and stood easily, still grinning at him.

He pulled his hand back quickly, trying to ignore how right her smaller hand had felt in his. What was he thinking? He helped all manner of women around the world, but if they were married, even if their husbands were despicable scum balls, he was very careful not to cross any boundaries or have untoward thoughts. He'd controlled himself even around the gorgeous Malory Grange when she'd been married to that loser Senator Ted Malouf. After she was divorced, Gray had made his play and had been shot down by a woman for the first time in his life. But if he could control himself around the likes of Malory, he could definitely keep himself from feeling attracted to Scarlett.

Scarlett Lily Quinn was one of the top A-list actresses in the world. He'd known her for years, hosted the Grammy awards with her, and had run into her at numerous events and parties. Her husband, Griff, was a tough ex-Navy SEAL who Gray had been impressed with, the furthest thing from a scum ball. Scarlett was expecting their second child; Gray thought she was due soon. He looked and her stomach was far too flat to be anywhere close to expecting. She looked fit in tight black clothing that outlined her lean frame and all her curves. Very, very fit. And he shouldn't be looking at her like that. He scrubbed at his beard with his fingertips.

"Close, but no cigar," Scarlett drawled. "Sara Sanderson. I'm Scarlett's stunt double."

"Oh. That's right." Relief filled him. He wasn't attracted to a married woman. *Thank you, heaven, above.* But Scarlett's stunt double ... interesting. Very interesting.

He still had no clue why she was here or why Tim or one of his other security people weren't rushing out here to intercept her. He stared at Sara's beautiful face with her startling blue eyes and smooth, dark hair. It was incredible how much she and Scarlett looked alike, except for the eye and hair color. Did Sara dye her hair, or wear a wig for her stunts? Colored contacts, or did they not really get close enough to show a stunt double's eye color?

"We met in ..." He was grappling. He remembered meeting her. Very well. But he traveled so often that most of the locations blended together. It had been tropical. An incredibly lush jungle. The cloud forest. A high-profile wedding. A benefit concert.

"Costa Rica," she supplied. "Colt Quinn and Kim Heathrow's wedding, and you did a benefit concert for Jex and Pearl Steele's extreme sports camp for the refugees' children."

He nodded, all the pieces clicking. She remembered their first meeting; he liked that. She'd been beautiful, sassy, and grinning then as well. He'd felt an instant attraction to her but hadn't seen her since, and finding her phone number had proven tougher than he'd imagined it would be. That had been a couple years ago, and he'd been busy composing songs, playing on his saxophone or the keyboard, recording songs, and traveling on tours like the one he just finished and the one he was set to start in a couple weeks. At least the Caribbean would be a short tour.

"It's good to see you," he said.

"It's good to be seen." She winked and looked over him. "You're looking *fabulous,* as always."

"Thank you." He was pretty sure she was teasing him, not flirting with him. He resisted flexing to make sure she knew how hard he worked to look 'fabulous.' He stayed extremely fit with both his own personal trainer and a world-renowned chef who traveled with him and cooked healthy and delicious food.

"You're not going to return the compliment?" She flipped her long, dark hair over her shoulder and winked.

He laughed. She was irresistible. It was the same impression he'd had last time he'd met her. No wonder he'd tried so hard to track down her number. But Scarlett had insisted she couldn't give Sara's number out to any of the many men who asked. He'd hated that response, and even his impressive assistant Janie had struck out. But Janie was always jealous of any woman he was interested in, so he suspected she hadn't tried as hard as she should.

"You look even more gorgeous than last time I saw you. Your beautiful face is more exquisite and mind-blowing than the sunrise over the Jungfrau."

"Ah." She patted his cheek and said almost condescendingly, "That smooth tongue of yours. Maybe if you wrote a song about me, I'd believe you were sincere."

He chuckled. "All right. Challenge accepted." He shivered, the cold wind brushing over his half-clothed and wet body. His temperature was dropping, and quick. The water still dripping from his suit had gone from warm to freezing. He'd probably gotten her wet from pinning her down, but she didn't shiver or act cold.

"Let's get you inside," she said, tilting her head toward the glass doors.

He gestured for her to go first. Sara smiled and shook her head. "Gentlemen," she said in a scoffing tone.

His eyebrows rose. What was that about? He had a lot of questions for her. But first ... "How did you get past my security guy?"

"Oh, Tim?" She looked back at Gray. "He's fine, but he is duct-taped and zip-tied next to the garage."

"Excuse me?" He stared at her, pretty certain she was joking, but admittedly not a hundred percent. His security guys were top-notch, and he couldn't imagine Russ not coming himself if an intruder had penetrated his intricately woven security web. No matter how gorgeous and welcome this intruder was.

"I'd tell you to go look, but you need to get dressed, and wading through that snow might give you frostbite. It's freezing out here." She did the cutest all-over body shiver he'd ever seen. Maybe cute was the wrong word. He could write an entire song about how appealing she looked right now. "I know, I'm gorgeous. I can read it in your eyes, and yes, you did get me wet pinning me down." Shaking her head and laughing at him, she said, "Come on, my irresistible saxophone player and singer extraordinaire. Let's go." She bounced to the patio door and flung it wide, slipping inside.

Gray grabbed a towel and hurried after her, squeezing some of the water out of his suit before securing the towel around his waist. He shut the door behind him, appreciating the warm house, the in-floor heating making even the wood floor warm. She walked over to the fireplace, picked up the remote, and clicked it on.

"Nice place," she said, giving a cursory glance around at the three-story open area with the massive three-story stone fireplace on the wall next to the double doors to the master suite. The wall perpendicular to that was three levels of windows overlooking the valley almost two thousand feet below, the huge living room and state-of-the-art kitchen and dining area on the opposite side of the windows. The 'nice place' was a twenty-million-dollar mansion perched on an exclusive mountainside a short walk from the high-dollar resort village of Wengen and one of the most gorgeous settings in the world, but it didn't seem to impress this lady much.

"Thanks," he murmured. He was so confused right now. Why was Scarlett Lily's stunt double in his living room, teasing and flirting with him, and had she truly bested his highly trained security guards? If that was true, why had she let Gray pin her down? He thought himself a great fighter, but he hadn't bested even Kaden yet, despite the tips Tim always gave him when they sparred, and Russ and Cameron were ten times tougher than Kaden. Russ was a decorated and accomplished retired Marine who Gray thought would win a battle against any man or woman in the world.

"Come over here and get warm," she said again. "I've got a bit to tell you and then you can shower while I get settled. Then we'll chat more, as I'm sure the questions will keep coming."

"Did you really tie Tim up?" he asked in disbelief, walking to the fireplace and getting in her space, staring down at her beautiful and seemingly innocent face. Up close, her exquisite blue eyes that seemed so lit up and friendly were actually guarded. He'd met and helped many, many women over the years and could usually read what they needed and the anguish they'd been through. This woman had a shield up that he doubted anyone could get through.

"Zip-tied and duct taped," she corrected in a sing-song tune. "Of course I did. The rest of your security men are equally incapacitated. You're right. We should go say hello to them quick and let them go. They can go free Tim. He was dressed in high-quality gear but he might be getting chilled with the lack of movement. I needed to prove a point," she grinned and shrugged, "but I examined the surrounding area and put up extra perimeter security when I disabled yours. I'll know if anyone but me tries to infiltrate your beautiful rental home, but it's probably not smart to leave your guys out of commission with all the people you have after you at the moment. Plus, if I'm going to be working with your security, I shouldn't make enemies out of them. I might get my hand slapped for that one."

Sara was equal parts gorgeous, appealing, cute, baffling, and possibly unstable. Hand slapped? Did she ever get in trouble for her sassy tongue and antics? Who could get upset at a woman with a smile that friendly, sweet, and innocent? Though if she'd truly bested his security, she was light years from sweet.

He had so many questions, but he started with, "All the people after me?" He scrubbed his fingers through his beard. "The Russian mafia?"

"Yes, but they aren't the most worrisome party at the moment. You like to tick people off, don't you?"

His eyes widened. He ticked bad people off when he helped those who needed him, but most of the world loved him and his music.

"Come on. Sorry to put off your shower and getting warm, but you do look mighty fine in that swimming suit." Sara's voice was still lilting and happy, as if she were teasing or laughing at him at all times. He couldn't imagine any world where this small and innocent-looking woman could take out his well-trained security. She must have other operatives hiding somewhere outside.

"Who's working with you?" he asked, looking around.

"We'll get into that soon, but for the moment, I'm here alone."

She turned and walked toward the stairs. No, this woman didn't know how to simply walk. She bounced or danced or skipped. With each step she lifted slightly onto tiptoe. Her hair floated around her shoulders, and she pranced to the stairs and down them. Gray was certain he'd never been around a more fascinating woman in his life. He'd thought he was in love with Malory Grange for almost a year and a half, regularly begging her to marry him, but Malory had shockingly found and married her former fiancé two weeks ago. He'd imagined it would hurt more, but he knew now that Malory had always been in love with Van Udy. Gray had helped her escape her horrific ex, Senator Ted Malouf. He was happy for her. Even Malory hadn't held the appeal Sara did, and he hardly knew Sara.

They descended the stairs and walked into the massive basement. It had its own kitchen and living section, four bedrooms, a workout room, and a separate theater. The carpet was warm with the radiant, in-floor heating on here as well. It felt good on his toes. Sara looked over her shoulder and for a brief second her gaze focused on his chest, her cheeks turned a becoming pink, and she tripped over something.

Gray reached out a hand and steadied her. She stilled under his touch, and he found himself wrapping his hand around her waist and slowly tugging her toward him. She stared up at him, all traces of laughter and teasing replaced with a warmth that made his heart race faster than when she'd knocked him down on the patio.

She rested her palms on his shoulders. The warmth seared into his bare skin. Gray let out a telling groan and focused on her summer-sky blue eyes. Her gaze captured him completely, and lyrics raced through his head. He was lost and found in her gaze. Her touch lit a fire in him he'd never known existed outside of song lyrics and romance novels.

"Mpmf!" A strangled yell came from across the room, and a body scooted from behind the pool table.

"Cameron?" Gray questioned, stunned by what he was seeing. His tough bodyguard. Incapacitated. Just as she'd said. Zip ties secured the man's hands behind his back and to his feet, which were also secured together. His mouth was covered with duct tape.

"Apologies." Sara's grin was back and that teasing, almost-mocking light filled her blue eyes. She pulled from Gray's grasp and strode toward Cameron, pulling a knife out of her pocket and flipping it open.

Russ and Kaden stormed out of the bedroom they'd converted into their security headquarters. Russ's face and neck were mottled red, the skin around his mouth raw and patches of his beard missing. His dark eyes were furious. Kaden was actually smiling, but the kid had a perma-grin and he didn't have a beard, so maybe he wasn't as upset about the effects of the duct tape.

"Ah, good job." Sara straightened and faced the two security guys who would make most people run the other direction if they were marching their way. She held the knife loosely in her hand. "You two get gold stars. Did you both get free, or did one of you free the other one?"

Russ reached her first and knocked the knife from her hand. It skittered across the nearby countertop. "I broke the zip ties."

He reached out with both hands, blood dripping from one wrist, most likely from his struggle with the zip ties, and moved to grasp her upper arms. Sara knocked his hands away, dodged underneath his arms, landed a vicious punch to his kidneys, and then she leaped and kicked him in the side of the head. Russ stuttered but straightened quickly.

"Gray," Russ grunted out. "Move away while we take care of this problem."

"Stand down, Russ," Gray commanded. "Do you know who this is?"

"I don't care if she's the President. She incapacitated and took down my men. By herself."

She really was alone and had taken out his security? What in the world? He'd never been so impressed, confused, and interested in a woman.

"I don't hit women," Russ growled at Sara. "So you still have the advantage, but you got the drop on me last time and knocked Kaden out cold so quietly I have to know how you did it. I will have you hogtied and answering some questions."

"Russ!" Gray sharpened his voice. "You work for me, and you will keep your hands off of her." He'd never talked to Russ, any of his security, or probably anybody since dealing with high school bullies, like that. But even his respected stepdad would have to be called out and stopped if he wanted to hogtie this woman.

Sara gave Gray a sweet smile. "Ah, that's so cute. You trying to protect me, Smokey G? Just like you protect every beautiful woman who flutters her eyelashes at you?" She fluttered her eyelashes, and it was an enticing move on her part. If only it hadn't been done sarcastically.

Gray's chest tightened. Did she realize the danger she was in? Russ was obviously ticked, and no way could she best him and Kaden at the same time. Especially without the element of surprise to aid her. He didn't like the derogatory way she'd referred to his propensity to protect women in danger. He personally thought it was one of his best qualities, but she seemed to be making fun of him.

"Thank you, sweet boy," she said, pumping her eyebrows at him. "But I don't need your protection."

Sweet boy? Wow. She was a smart aleck to the tenth degree.

She looked at Russ. "I took you down once, tough guy, I'll do it again. Oh, and so sorry about the beard. It looks awful, by the way." She patted him on the cheek before darting away.

Russ let out a roar and lunged after her. Kaden came around to his other side. The two men were huge, and despite her obviously impressive training, skills, and bravado, it had to be terrifying to see these bodyguards coming at her like that.

Gray rushed to protect her. He wouldn't let any woman be hurt while he was there to keep her safe.

Sara squatted and used Russ's shoulders to launch herself into the air. It looked like a move from an action movie. She kicked Russ in the head again and he knocked into Kaden. Then she flipped and landed next to Gray. Scrambling behind him and onto his back, she wrapped both legs around his waist and one arm so tight around his neck he was immediately gasping for air. A pistol materialized in her hand, and she shoved it into his temple.

Russ and Kaden were rushing their way, but they both froze. They looked angry enough to chew up and spit out nails. But they also looked helpless, which he'd never seen out of his security team. Russ's eyes were desperate. He'd do anything to keep Gray safe. Gray knew Russ had made a deathbed promise to his mom to protect her only son with his life.

The room went cold, despite the warm woman wrapped around him from behind. This was no romantic move. Sara was tough, crazy, an impressive fighter, and she was going to kill him. Gray had assumed because of her association with Scarlett Lily that she was a good person and had stupidly let her into his house.

He wasn't sure why she hadn't killed him outside, but he suspected she was enjoying the game and ridiculing all of them before finishing them off.

At the moment, he didn't have time to philosophize about her motives or how tough, accomplished, and insane she was. She must've been sent by the mafia or maybe by that crazy Princess Byoode to kill him. It didn't look like Russ or Kaden could intervene before she pulled the trigger. Could he talk her out of killing his men?

His life flashed before his eyes. He'd helped a lot of people, especially women in danger, but he had no family left, no legacy but his music and his money to leave behind. Was this how it would end for him?

"Please," he croaked out. She was letting in just enough oxygen to keep him from passing out. "Kill me if that's your objective, but let my men go."

"No. Don't kill him," Russ barked, desperation making his voice even rougher. "We'll do anything you want."

"Please," Gray repeated. He appreciated Russ and knew he truly would do anything for him, but if this woman was going to kill him, there wasn't much hope of him living through a bullet in his brain. "These men aren't part of your hit. You'll still get paid by whoever sent you, and you won't have four great men's deaths on your hands as well." He sucked in another shallow breath. "If there's any humanity left in you, please let them live."

The room went quiet. Sara held tightly to him, but she quivered slightly. Russ and Kaden stared at him in horror. He could see

Cameron out of the corner of his eye, struggling to move around the pool table and get closer, even though he was bound.

He focused on his stepdad. The man's dark eyes were full of frustration and despair. He couldn't handle letting Gray die after they'd both lost Gray's mom. Gray understood Russ's anguish, but this was a sacrifice Gray would make every time.

Cameron, Tim, and Kaden would also give their lives for his. He knew they would. But right now, it was his turn to take that burden.

Gray waited for her to pull the trigger, praying that she'd honor his request and his last act would at least preserve the four men who had protected and served him and their country. He wasn't ready to die, but there were worse things. He'd see his mom and meet his Savior soon. That was a comforting thought. All of his billions were earmarked for Jex and Pearl Steele's charities. His money would help many children throughout the world.

It wasn't the worst way to end his sojourn on the earth.

As long as Sara let his men live.

Find *Matchmaking the Singer and the Warrior* on Amazon.

FIVE FREE BOOKS

Download the complete Echo Ridge Romance Collection here when you sign up for Cami's newsletter.

Christmas Makeover:

Chelsea Jamison has been infatuated with Drew Stirling longer than she's loved playing basketball, high-top sneakers, and the Knicks. Unfortunately, all Drew sees is the kid who kicked his trash in the high school free throw contest and not the girl whose heart breaks into a fast dribble when he's near.

Drew makes an unexpected visit home to Echo Ridge and their friendship picks up where they left off as they scheme to make a teenaged boy's Christmas dreams come true. When Chelsea realizes she's fallen for her best friend, she wonders if there is any hope of a relationship with Drew or if she's stuck in buddy-status for life.

Last of the Gentlemen:

Despite the hardships she's faced, Emma Turner is determined to make a good life for her three children. Working nights and struggling through life doesn't leave much time for romance, which is just fine as far as Emma is concerned. But when her son's good-looking lacrosse coach takes an interest in her children, Emma has to fight off the smolder in her stomach and banish her daydreams. This schoolgirl crush needs to end before she embarrasses her son and herself. If only she could tell that to her heart.

My Best Man's Wedding:

Jessica Porter made a vow to marry her best guy friend, Josh, when they turned thirty. When Josh calls with the news that he's coming home to Echo Ridge for his wedding, Jessica is determined to break up the happy couple and take her rightful place as his bride. Gentry Trine, a coworker, agrees to pretend to be her fiancé to stir up feelings of jealousy. However, Jessica didn't realize fake fiancés could kiss like champions, and make a girl smile nonstop. Can she figure out which is the right man for her before she loses them both?

Change of Plans:

Kaitlyn knows who she's destined to spend her life with, until superstar Axel Olsen turns her dreams upside down.

Kaitlyn Johanson is chosen by heartthrob, nationally-acclaimed lacrosse player, Axel Olsen, for a dream date. She didn't know a man touching her hand could feel like heaven, but she awkwardly blacks out then admits to him that she's in a relationship.

Kaitlyn comes home to Echo Ridge hoping to rekindle her relationship with her high school boyfriend, Mason. She never expects Axel to show up in her hometown, hosting a lacrosse camp with Mason and his stepdad.

When Axel steals her attention and possibly her heart from the man she is supposed to marry, she has to decide if she'll take a risk on new love or give old love a second chance.

Counterfeit Date:

Mason Turner only has eyes for Lolly Honeymiller. She's vivacious and hilarious and unfortunately thinks of him as her best friend's ex. Lolly's friends cook up a scheme: pretending Lolly is making him over for a special date with his dream girl. The more time he and Lolly spend together, the harder it is to keep his feelings a secret.

Lolly offers to help Mason Turner prepare for a date with his dream girl. Through makeovers, shopping, and practice kissing, she tries to keep her distance but finds herself falling for a man she can never have. As the date approaches, both wonder if they can keep things fake or if the farce will implode and shred both of their hearts.

Download your free copy here.

Made in United States
North Haven, CT
04 March 2023